Four Ways To Midnight:
An Anthony Carrick Short Story Collection

By

Jason Blacker

PUBLISHED BY:
Lemon Tree Publishing
JasonBlacker.com

ISBN: 9781927623510

For my wife, without you the world is dark

Table of Contents

Money Ain't Nothing

Damn mosquitoes and it wasn't even summer. They kept going at it. I opened my eyes and realized it was my cell. Vibrating and gyrating like a nubile belly dancer. I fumbled for it plopping my hand in the ashtray. What the hell, I decided to cross myself. Remember man thou art dust...damn phone kept buzzing. I grabbed at it as it tried to skitter off the table.

"Hello," I said looking at my clock radio. Six thirty in the morning. What's wrong with people.

"Is this Mr. Carrick. Mr. Anthony Carrick?"

The voice was soft and sad, like rain clouds over the ocean.

"Yes."

A bit of awkward silence so I figured I might as well close my eyes and take a nap.

"I need your help. You're a detective right?"

"No, not really. Detectives work for the police. I'm just a gumshoe."

"A what?"

"Okay ma'am, I'm a detective but I'm not a cop."

I straightened up now. The sheet fell off my chest like my last lover. It was cold in here. No wonder, it was too damn early for a conversation.

"Is this a bad time Mr. Carrick?"

The k sounded like a slammed door right in my ear.

"Not any more," I said. I rubbed my eyes. Someone had put salt and pepper in them the night before. I took a deep breath and reached for my cigarettes.

"Listen, I just called to ask for your help. I'm sorry I bothered you."

I waited a second to see if she'd hang up. Actually I was stuffing a Marlboro in my mouth.

"Now wait just a minute. Didn't say I wouldn't help. It's just that I'm not a morning person that's all."

A sigh on the other end not unlike that of a lover. I liked her already. She was slim and good looking with pouty red lips. But I get confused.

"Mr. Carrick, my son's dead."

She stopped there to gauge my reaction. Funny thing is they usually all are by the time I get the call. A fixer-upper with nothing left to fix, only rot to cover up and plaster over.

"Sorry to hear that. Call me Anthony."

I lit my cigarette away from the phone. I didn't want to be rude. I inhaled and felt a lot better.

"Captain John Roberts told me you could help. He said that he knew you, or knows you. Anyway, he said you were good."

"Yes I know John Ms.?"

"It's Marlene Greenlaub. Anyway, he said that you could help. That you would help as a favor to him."

Yeah the only reason he'd say that was because he wanted her off his damn back. That John, always looking out for me.

I tipped my cigarette into the ashtray. The ash fell off and lay like an inukshuk. Nice word that. Just found out about that the other day from a Canadian fella on the TV.

"I start at five hundred bucks a day Marlene. Plus expenses. But sometimes people don't think they get their money's worth."

I hadn't worked in a while and I sure could use the money. But if Johnny said I'd help her out I figured I might as well save her the money. Nothing doing usually in the cases he sends me.

"I have the money Mr. Carrick. More than enough. When can I meet you?"

The voice was crisper now. Maybe my hearing was better. Maybe she was a class above me. I looked at the clock again. It was leaning towards six forty five and I was leaning towards breakfast.

"How about seven thirty at Joe's Main Diner. You know where it is?"

"No I don't Mr. Carrick. I live up on Mulholland Drive."

She kept calling me Mr. Carrick. I liked it but I knew what she meant. Some folks call you mister out of respect. I get that sometimes. Other folks call you mister because you're hired help. She figured I was hired help. I figured she'd earn my respect.

"I'm sure your fancy car can figure it out with that new fangled GPS they got now."

I hung up on her. I didn't need the money that bad. But I looked at my empty scotch glass longingly. No way the sun was past the yardarm. Not even in Tuktoyaktuk. That's another word I heard from that Canadian I was telling you about. A city or something I think. I took another drag of my cigarette and ash fell on my chest. I moved over slowly to the ashtray and brushed it out of my hair. Didn't work too good. Flakes fell like pepper all over the side table. Ruining the dram of scotch I was going to use as mouthwash.

I took a last drag and then squashed out my cigarette, turned to get out of bed. Forgot about something and blew smoke rings at the window. I watched them open their mouths all surprised-like until something warm and furry rubbed itself against my shin.

"Pirate," I said looking down at the most beat up cat you ever saw. Studied but never graduated in the sweet science. That's when I found him. But that's another story. A good one for sure, but for another time. I heard a growl but it wasn't from Pirate. I rubbed my belly, got up and went to the bathroom.

The shower was good. So was the other stuff. How do they call that, ablutions or something. Went into the kitchen and threw some food into Pirate's dog bowl. Only my aim wasn't so good so I bent over to pick up the fallen pieces. He ate hungrily. I liked that.

"That's my boy Pirate," I said to him. Not many teeth left but that didn't bother him. He preferred swallowing to chewing. Like father like son I guess. I went into the bedroom and got changed. I threw on a nice crisp shirt, just in case Marlene showed up. I picked up my fedora and headed out the door, giving Pirate a scratch behind the ears.

"Be a good boy," I said. He always was.

Joe's Main Diner is a great little place down on Main Street here in Santa Monica. A little hole in the wall. But in the best sense. Only a few of us locals know about it. And the best thing about it is it's only about fifteen minutes or so walk from my place. It has a great big tree in front of it. The kind that boys will climb. In the country that is. Or maybe in a different era.

I took my usual spot against the wall. A two seater. Maybe I was expecting company.

"Hi ya Mr. Carrick. The usual?" asked the waitress.

"Thanks hun. Why don't you call me Anthony?"

She twiddled with her fingers looking at them. And then she did a kind of bounce or curtsy.

"I dunno. I guess you kinda remind me of my dad."

She looked at me shyly. I gave her wink. "Okay hun," I said. Jesus, kids nowadays. A guy wears a shirt and a hat and they figure he's gramps. Yeah I could be old enough to be her dad. Only if she was jailbait and I hadn't even been a man yet.

I looked around the joint. A few regulars I knew. A few strays. I looked out at the tree. No kids climbing it. I looked at my cell and it said seven thirty. I looked up again towards the door - something catching my eye. A tall woman not from around these parts. She wore a long blue dress. The kind that sashayed just because you looked at it. Her hair was in blonde curls and I could see them resting on my pillow. Yeah, she was tall and good looking but no pouty lips. Two out of three ain't bad so the song says. She saw me looking at her and made her way over.

"Here's your coffee Anthony," said the kid.

"You're a doll. Not so hard hey?" she smiled and went off to another table.

"Mr. Carrick," said the woman. There was that door slamming k.

"Yes," I said. I stood up. I couldn't help myself. Old school. Years of inbreeding. Call it what you want.

"Have a seat." She did. So did I. Two packets of sugar and a splash of milk later and I smiled at her over my coffee. She was punctual. That counted for a lot.

"It's Marlene, Mr. Carrick. Marlene Greenlaub." She said Marlene around an imaginary egg in her mouth. It was putting me off her.

"I figured Marlene."

"You're not one for pleasantries are you Mr. Carrick?"

"Sorry. Let's start again. Would you like something to eat?"

"No."

"Listen Marlene. Some people rub me the wrong way. I'm like an alley cat and you're like a pampered poodle. Maybe you have the wrong man."

I sipped my coffee and she put her purse on the table. She fumbled in it and grabbed a packet of cigarettes. She toyed with them. Rubbing the packet slowly with immaculate hands. I liked her again. I sympathized with her. These bleeding hearts in SoCal wouldn't let you have a smoke anywhere nowadays. Trying to save everybody from themselves. I took my pack out and placed it close to hers. It was more boxy. Hers was fancy. Called themselves "Lady Slims". She pulled up the top and the filters were red. Like her lipstick, like her fingernails. Like my blood.

My French toast came out with glassy, brown fried banana on it. I could smell the dough. Yeasty like beer.

"Would you like a menu ma'am?" the waitress asked Marlene. I looked at her. Her razor red lips said no. Nothing at all. I figured this wasn't her kind of place. Too bad. The food's good.

"Maybe you're right Mr. Carrick. But John Roberts said you're the best outside the police department. So did Chief Burton."

I put a forkful of food in my mouth and a swig of coffee.

"You're misinformed Ms. Greenlaub. I'm the best inside and outside of the department."

She raised an eyebrow at me. I raised her two.

"Frank Burton said you were a tough nut. But you don't look like one."

"I get that a lot. Must be my boyish good looks."

Despite Marlene's acid, my food tasted really good. She was missing out. I looked across at a young couple sharing some eggs. The hippie types. Birkenstock sandals and beaded hair. Kids nowadays.

"Well Mr. Carrick. Are you interested in hearing what I've got to say?"

She was playing with her pack of cigs. Flipping it around on its edge. I couldn't keep my eyes off her hands. I could see them doing things. Doing things I shouldn't say.

"I'm all ears."

The waitress came by and filled up my coffee. I was getting alert. I looked at Marlene. She was looking at her cigarettes. Her eyes were wet, glassy.

"My son Mr. Carrick is dead." I felt some déjà vu. "He was found yesterday evening at our home. Captain Roberts came by personally. He thinks it's an unintentional death. Accidental." She took the napkin and blotted her eyes.

"John's not often wrong," I said. I pushed my plate forward. I was losing my appetite seeing a woman get misty on me.

"I'm sorry Marlene, you might be wasting your time and money with me. I'd bet dollars to donuts that he's likely right." I was trying to console her.

She looked at me steady. Stealing a gaze at my soul, but it was hiding pretty good.

"You're an honest man Mr. Carrick. John told me about that too."

"Did he tell you about my lonely childhood and lack of affection from my mother?" I was being facetious. Sometimes I just can't help myself. She chose to overlook that. Good for her.

"I just want a second opinion that's all. He's my first born son Mr. Carrick. You don't know what that's like. I'd just like you to have a look. Please. Money's not important. I need your help for my own sanity Mr. Carrick. I trust John and he vouches for you. That's good enough for me."

She bit her lip and left red lipstick on her teeth. Her eyes were wet. I'm a sucker for a damsel in distress.

"I'll help you. But I'll tell you upfront it probably won't change things." She nodded.

"Thank you Mr. Carrick."

"I take twenty five hundred upfront, a five day minimum. Five hundred a day, plus expenses. Like this breakfast here. But this one's on me."

She dug into her purse again. Goddamn hands, I really liked those hands. She pulled out twenty five Benjamins and put them on my cigarette pack. Looked like she had picked them up from the Reserve on her way over. I could smell the money from here.

"Here's my card Mr. Carrick," she placed it on Benjamin's face, "please look into my son's girlfriend. Her name is Melodie Rimes. My son took out a quarter million insurance policy on himself two weeks ago payable to her. I don't like her Mr. Carrick. She's trash and no good. Please be in touch."

She got up to go. I placed my hand on her forearm. It was warm and soft. She looked at my hand.

"Your son's name Ms. Greenlaub?"

"William. William Greenlaub." She patted my hand and walked out the diner. I watched her light a cigarette outside. A blue jewel with red highlights. She inhaled that cigarette lovingly and then a black limo pulled up. She climbed in and was gone. I swallowed hard. I thought about scotch again. I thought about a lot of other things too. I got up and put on my fedora. I put a cigarette in my mouth and left Alex on the table with some silver friends. I walked out into the hazy day. I could smell the ocean. And I could see dead people. Too many dead people. I lit my cigarette and walked towards the pier. Marlene's fragrance in my nose.

I sat on a bench on Ocean Front watching tourists getting off big buses and strolling towards the pier. Wearing cameras around their necks like gangsta bling bling. I fished out my phone and Marlene's card. Marlene Greenlaub it said. 555-2640. That's all. Nice card though. Soft red and light blues. I saw that dress sashaying again. I saw those blonde curls on my pillow. Damnit Anthony focus. I called an old friend.

"John it's Anthony."

"Anthony pal, what's happening?"

"A foxy lady named Marlene you sent my way. Why'd you do it?"

"I figured you could use the money buddy. By the way, you ever gonna come back?"

"I doubt it." A Chinese lady was trying to take my picture. Or so it looked like. Philip Marlowe she said to her husband pointing at me. I looked around but I didn't see him. I was flattered though.

"Well they'll take you back in a minute old friend."

"Say, you got some time to talk about Marlene."

"Sure come on over to my office. I'll see you in about an hour?"

"Make it two. You know traffic in L.A."

"Good stuff."

I hung up and looked around for Marlowe again. I could use his help. He wasn't there and the Chinese lady was gone. I blew smoke rings again only they were buffeted around by the slow, easy salty breeze. I saw a Paris wannabe clutching a small dog in her elbow. That's why I love this place. A freak show everyday.

John was working up at the North Hollywood station on Burbank Boulevard. I'd been there a few times. That was a while back. Two hours should be plenty. I draped my arm over the bench watching fit folks run around. A couple of nice looking young ladies roller bladed by in bikini tops. Wasn't that hot out. And you could tell too. But I didn't mind that. I squashed out my cigarette in the ashtray. I could smell the salty air again and I figured it was time to get going. I made my way back to my apartment.

Pirate was sunning himself in a rectangular piece of sun. He looked at me with one eye as I left again. I got into my car and headed up to North Hollywood. Traffic was raging on both the I-10 and I-405. I didn't have my Glock with me. Good thing too. This kind of traffic leads a man to distraction. It took me over an hour to get there. But then I remembered my Benjamins riding with me and it didn't feel so bad. I parked my LeSabre across the street and walked into the government building. They don't win any architectural prizes for police buildings.

"Hey Anthony how are ya?" asked Tony Montana.

"Good thanks. I'm looking for John. Can you go wake him for me?"

I took a seat and waited. An old lady was filling out an accident form. She looked too old to be driving, but who am I to say.

"Hey Anthony, come on back to my office," said John.

I followed him into a closet with a desk and cabinet. I was impressed. This is why we get so much work done. He pulled in another chair and we were sitting elbows to ribs.

"What can you share with me about this Greenlaub thing?"

John reached into the black filing cabinet and pulled out a thin manila folder. He opened it up on the desk. There were some pictures up on top. One was of William lying in the bathtub like he was having a bath. But there was no water in it. His body had a grayish tint. There were a couple of larger red marks over his chest. His eyes were closed. That's always best.

"This is how he was found. As close as we know. His brother found him when he came home. Our victim had been home alone for the afternoon. We figure he was probably dead a couple of hours before he was found. But the coroner will confirm that."

"What's that prick there on his arm?" I pointed to a needle mark on his left arm this side of the elbow. "Did he do drugs?"

"That's why I wanted to call you in Anthony. See, we have to be discreet whereas you don't. We're looking into that. It looks fairly fresh but we can't be sure. Haven't asked Ms. Greenlaub about that. Could be a sore point, so we're waiting on the coroner again."

"What's your hunch?"

"I don't have a hunch Anthony, you should know better than that. But it wouldn't surprise me. We see a lot of wealthy kids toying with smack and shit like that."

"How did he die?"

"Don't know for sure. Looks like he might have slipped in the bathtub and cracked his head. Or maybe he just knocked himself out and then drowned. That'd be my guess. These red splotches over his chest are probably from the hot water beating down. I'm not certain this was a murder Anthony, despite the insurance policy for Melodie."

"So she wasn't known to you?"

"Most folks like this are known to us. But just petty juvenile stuff. Shoplifting etc."

"Have you spoken to her?"

"No, not yet. You know our workloads here. We're getting to it. Doesn't look like a homicide like I said. But then again, you seem to find homicides out of little old ladies passing on in their sleep."

He grinned at me and spread the pics around. Some of the scene. The bath tub. The fancy bathroom with marble sink which needed a clean. Little droplets of water around and some dirty, smudged droplets around the sink. The pale blue towel was a little smudged in parts. I asked John about that. He figured the guy had washed his hands before he had a shower. Didn't want to dirty the shower taps first. Fair enough I said. It was his own bathroom and teenagers aren't sticklers for cleanliness. The bathmat was crumpled up. Probably the brother. They never pay attention to scene contamination when they find loved ones. Understandable. Couple of droplets of water on the floor here and there. Some Alfred Sung cologne on the counter. Barely used. Toothpaste with whitener and these fancy sonic toothbrushes. All a façade. Where was the depth? No blood spilling out from behind the head that I could see. Might have been washed away. I asked John about that. No blood at the scene he said.

"You mind if I talk to this Melodie?" "I was hoping you'd say that. Would be a big help to us?"

He scribbled her name and number on a sticky note. Doctor's handwriting. I wouldn't have been able to read it if I didn't have chicken scratch myself.

"Still no penmanship classes at the academy?"

He grinned at me. "You're a fine one to talk. Maybe you could come back and give some pointers."

I shook my head. I'd been gone too long. And I left for a reason. I wasn't coming back.

"Tempting though," I said.

I like John but I was too close to him. I could smell his cheap cologne. Sweet like flowers, like something old men might wear at those clubs you see them at sometimes looking down the shirts of young women. John wasn't married. I figured a wife wouldn't let him wear stuff like that. And he wasn't old. Not old enough to be interested in young women.

"How's the chief?" I asked him rolling my chair towards the closet door to get some fresh air.

"He knows you've been invited onto the case. He says good things about you. Can't figure out why you took in that mangy cat though."

"Birds of a feather, or something like that. But he wouldn't know about that."

I looked at the folder again. I was still close enough. I looked at another picture of William. High school grad photo. Good looking kid with blonde curls like his mother. But his lips were full, not sharp and he had a lazy eye. The left one was half closed as he smiled.

"How old was he?"

John rifled through some of the papers clipped to the back of the folder.

"Nineteen," he said, "full life ahead of him."

"Maybe," I said, "maybe he wasn't going to amount to much."

John grinned again. He does that. Finds the oddest things funny. I got up from the chair. I wanted to smell the salty air again. I grabbed his paw and shook it tight. He didn't get up. He closed the folder and put it away and leaned back in his chair.

"Don't go cracking any heads now Anthony. This one needs to be discreet."

Now it was my turn to grin at him. I walked outside and stuck a cigarette in my face. I let it hang there cold. I got in my car and went for a drive. I figured the crime scene would be a place to start.

I parked on the shoulder of the road. I could get used to it up here. Nice and quiet, probably great views of the ocean. I figured their house was probably worth a few million. Maybe more. Hard to say for someone like me. Still, looked like too much house for three people. Maybe four if pops was still around. I lit my cigarette. The first puff bit my throat. I swallowed down a cough and pulled out my cell again. Signal was good, so I figured I'd call someone who might want to reminisce with me.

"Hello," it was a girl's voice. A little squeaky. Maybe like a mouse if they could talk.

"Melodie Rimes?" It was half a question.

"Yes."

"Melodie, this is Anthony Carrick. I'd like to talk to you about William."

"Who?" she was cute. But I gave her a chance.

"Pretty nice house they've got here. When can we meet?"

"I don't know what you're talking about Mr.?" She bit the bait. Her voice cracked a little like a porcelain doll. And it wasn't the line.

"Carrick honey, and I've been around these mean Mulholland streets to know a liar when I hear one. I'm easier to talk to than the cops. You might want to give me a try. Bring a tough guy with you if you'd like."

She didn't say much for a while so I blew smoke in her ear see if she'd like that.

"Okay Mr. Carrick."

"How about I come and see you?'

"Okay."

"Good then, where are you?"

"112 Culver City Terrace, just off of Playa Street. I'm not in trouble am I Mr. Carrick?"

Didn't sound like a question to me. So I lobbed it back at her.

"Should you be?" She didn't say anything to that. "I'll see you in about half an hour."

I was there as promised. I like being punctual. People know you mean business. I parked facing towards Playa Street. My nose pointing away from the mobile homes. There was a cemetery close by. Could come in handy. I walked along looking for 112. All these little homes packed up against each other. Nice and cozy. Some of them had potted plants outside. A burst of color, a nice distraction. But I'm being unkind. These folks mostly had pride of ownership as you hear about in the papers. But not so much 112. It was a sad looking building. Its face a frown. Paint faded and chipped here and there. A quarter mil could buy some space away from this place. Sure could. I squashed the buzzer on the doorframe. I heard the shrill ring like a big angry housewife. Nice and quick a young waif of a woman came to the door. Behind her trailed a Mexican looking fella in a wife beater. Her eyes had enough mascara to look beat up. Her hair was jet black and short all tousled. Goth I think is what they call it now. The Mexican fella was a thin short man with a prison buzz but no tattoos I could see. His hands were crossed in front of him, but it wasn't cold. He looked at me from a crooked neck.

"Mr. Carrick?" she said opening the door for me.

"Sure," I said as I took my hat off and entered the room. "Who's the hired help?" I pointed my hat at the Mexican.

He glared at me hard. It hurt my feelings but I got over it.

"That's Alvarez Sanchez the tough guy you said I should bring."

I invited myself in a little further. The carpet was stained and dirty. The couch with floral print was faded and worn. I could smell cat urine somewhere. I took a sniff off the couch before sitting down. It seemed okay. Melodie sat down across form me in a cheap armchair. Alvarez stood staring at me. I stared at him back. I got bored.

"Listen son, I didn't mean disrespect. I just don't take kindly to people looking at me like that."

He glared harder. I thought he might hurt himself so I took to looking at Melodie. She was easier on the eyes anyway.

"Tell me about Willy," I said. I couldn't help myself. Melodie glanced down at her hands and then at Alvarez.

"Do you need his permission to talk? Because I can come back later if you'd like."

"No…William was my boyfriend," she said. "We had a fight yesterday and I haven't heard from him since." She kept fidgeting with her hands. Alvarez shuffled a little bit and took his eyes from me for a second. He was getting tired.

"Have a seat son, this could take a while."

"What you gonna do huh pops," he said strutting his chin out at me.

"Well there's a lot of things I'd like to do, but that just gets me in trouble. Besides I'm tired and my breakfast left me sick. Worse than that I haven't had any liquor today and I'm just trying to keep ahead of the cops. You've got worse trouble than me coming son."

He took my advice like a good lad and had a seat. He still had his hands crossed but I could see them. Mechanic hands. Maybe he earned a living. His legs were wide out in front of him. Jutting towards me like wooden flotsam. I thought about breaking his kneecaps, just to relieve my frustration. But that would be too much trouble. I fished out another smoke instead.

"Can I have one?" she asked.

"Sure." This was going to be too easy. I tapped one out for her and she came up and got it. She had a young face. Maybe old enough to smoke. Pale white skin like a geisha. Maybe she was one. Maybe that's what got her into trouble. I lit it for her and she inhaled like she hadn't breathed in a long time. She was practiced. I offered Alvarez one but he shook his head real slow.

"Don't you want to know why I'm here?"

She looked at Alvarez and then said sure, why was I here? I told her she was making it too easy for me. I asked her about the quarter mil. She feigned ignorance. No Oscar for her.

"Well Willy had an insurance policy payable to you in case he died." She didn't mind that I bastardized his name like that.

"A quarter mil would sure get you and Alvarez a nice new start away from a place like this."

"Don't tell this dick nothing Melodie. He ain't nobody. He knows nothing." He glared at her this time and she looked between him and me. I smiled at her. Some folks murder people by accident. Those are the easiest to reel in. Like soft fat fish. They don't have the hardness needed. They're usually good people. Just got a bit of a temper. Terrible thing when it's not under control.

"Why did you do it Melodie? Just for the money. I don't figure you'd do it just for the money. You're not a mean girl. You could have waited and married him. Then you'd be in for a ton more."

"It's not like that," she said. I was taking candy from a baby.

"This is bullshit man. Don't say nothin' before you've called a lawyer," said Alvarez. She looked at him and then at me. I smiled at her again. I was feeling generous.

"She doesn't like me 'cos I'm from a trailer park. You don't know what it's like. She was always putting pressure on him to dump me. But he loved me okay. You probably don't get that either. I'd never kill him. Never. I couldn't collect the money if I had killed him anyway."

"How did you get him to buy life insurance? I'm curious. Why would a guy do that? Seems it would put him in a bit of a spot."

Alvarez was up and pacing. Cursing under his breath. Shit, shit, shit he kept saying. I was tired of playing with her. I wanted to pull her in. I looked at her a long while. I wasn't smiling anymore. As a matter of fact I was frowning. I'd practiced that look over the years. I took a pull on my Marlboro. The smoke stung my eyes and made me frown even more. She started playing with her fingers. Her cigarette growing ash. She couldn't look at me steady.

"Well," she said just glancing at me, "we figured, Billy and me, that if he had insurance for me then his mother would have to be more careful about trying to destroy us. We were in love okay. Not that you'd get it."

She was pouting at me now. Alvarez pacing around like a hungry panther trying to shut her up. I didn't buy what she was selling. Maybe because I didn't have enough.

"Come on Melodie stop playing with me. I get it that you were in love, but you don't seem like a bad girl. I'm sure you had your reasons. I just want to know. A lot of folks want to know. It'll give them closure. Think about his brother who had to find him."

"Don't say nothin' Mel. Nothin' you hear me?" He was glaring at her but it wasn't working so he turned it on me.

"What you playin' at pops? We ain't scared of you. You don't know nothin'"

"Sit down son. I said this could take a while. The way I see it, is one of you killed Will. I could believe it was an accident. I could even put a good word in for you to the cops and the D.A. We go back a ways."

I was running out of cigarette. I wanted to go someplace and have a long drink. I wasn't sure why I'd been handed this gig. Twenty five hundred bucks for too little work. So I wanted to finish this up.

"You know what I think Mel?" I could see Alvarez wince a bit at that. He didn't like it. "I think that Al over here did it. And you know why? Because his soiled hands were washed in the sink and he left his dirty paws all over the towel. That's what I think. Maybe I should just get going now. Send the cops out here to take a statement. Only they won't be so polite. These are rich folks you're dealing with. They've got connections. This is how cops get promoted on a slam dunk like this."

I made a show of getting up. Alvarez was tiring me out with all his pacing.

"Wait," said Melodie. I remained standing up, looking at Alvarez. He had his mitts thrust in his pockets now. He was slumping a little in the shoulders too. Like a sagging balloon. All his bravado leaving him with every breath.

"It was Alvarez's idea. He figured we could make some easy money after I told him hat Billy had taken an insurance policy out for me. He said he'd make it look like an accident, like he slipped in the bathtub or something, but I didn't want him to. I loved Billy okay. I didn't want him killed but I couldn't stop Alvarez."

She didn't look at him. She could hardly look at me. Alvarez was shaking his head back and forth. Shut up he was saying to her. You lying bitch he added. This was the best part. See how each of their stories unravels and you get to the truth.

She was lying. The way she didn't listen to Alvarez. The way she was trying to play coy with me from the beginning. The way she couldn't look at either of us decently. She was playing us both for a patsy, but I figured Alvarez wasn't going to go down like that. She was trying to play on prejudice. But I'd given up on that a while back. The more you see the seedy the more you realize it's a rotten core not stained skin.

"I don't know Alvarez. Does this seem real to you? I'm thinking that she figured that there'd be a way to make it look like an accident. And she played you for the patsy. Is that closer to anything like the truth?"

Alvarez came and sat back down. I took a seat on the same tired couch.

"What can you do for me if I tell the truth man?"

I told him I'd put in a good word. I told him I could see how a guy like him could be used by a pretty white girl like Melodie.

"Okay so this is how it went."

Melodie glared at him trying to hide the look. I caught it easily. A fly ball if there ever was one. I could taste the truth coming like a well aged scotch.

"Okay man. You're right about the towel. My hands were wet form trying to see if the guy was dead. Mel had gone over to see him. But the problem is she was two timing him with me. And she figured he didn't know, but he must've. Because after they had sex he told her he knew about me and that he was cancelling the insurance policy. He went to take a shower and she told me she got scared and angry. She went into the bathroom to plead with him. But he got mean and told her she was a no good trailer trash whore and that his mother had been right about her all along. He told her it was over and to get the fuck out of his house. She just lost it man and she pushed him as hard as she could when he wasn't looking. Then she called me and told me I had to get over there and when I did I couldn't feel a pulse on the guy. I washed my hands and turned the taps off and then we..."

Melodie got up and left the room. She looked mad. Looked like she was going to cry. I figured she was going to the bathroom to get some tissue. Alvarez never even noticed.

"We go the hell outta there. I was just happy to get going. I mean these were rich people like you say. I was nervous that the cops would come round anytime. I imagine they drive around these neighborhoods all the time. I grabbed Melodie and we bolted. She was cursing me and calling me a pathetic loser. Said we had to go back and straighten it out. Make it look like an accident. I told her it already looked like one and that I wasn't gonna get caught by the cops again. I've got a few juvy beefs but I'm straightening myself out. We came back here..."

I caught a glimpse of something in the corner of my eye. I turned to see Melodie carrying a small little black gun in both her hands. She was crying and the mascara was running down her cheeks in two thin triangles. I got up and moved to the side of the couch, just in case I had to jump in behind it. She was pointing what looked to me like a .32 caliber Tomcat at Alvarez.

"You stupid pathetic loser," she kept saying to him. Then there were two loud thunder claps and I looked over at him. Two little red poppies were growing on his chest. It wasn't Remembrance Day. And he had nothing left to remember.

"You don't know what it's like okay. You don't know what it's like. Nobody ever loved me. He was going to be my ticket out of this godforsaken place, if it wasn't for his damn mother and him finding out about Alvarez. But I would've ditched Alvarez. He just wouldn't give me chance...he wouldn't..."

She was getting hysterical now. The little Tomcat with a stubby nose eyeing me now with an unsteady gaze. I didn't like it. It was weaving back and forth in little smirks.

"The cops are coming Melodie. Do the right thing. Put the gun down and everything will be alright."

She was only about five feet away. I figured I could rush her if need be. Maybe she'd get a round off into my arm or leg. But I didn't want to try those Vegas odds. As I was thinking of options, with my hand out towards her offering my hat as a shield, she put the gun into her mouth. She kissed the gun good night at the sound of another crack. I didn't care too much for the mess she left on the far wall. I'd seen it too many times. Her body fell like a sack of potatoes at my feet and she lay down there. A trickle of red blood slipped out of her mouth and rolled onto the carpet. I didn't think these twenty five hundred bucks was so easy anymore. I started thinking maybe I had been played for the patsy.

I put on my fedora and walked out the front door. I closed it quietly after me. Out of respect. Some people had started poking their heads and bodies out of their homes. I walked on to my car. I called 911 and told them to get here quick and tell Captain John Roberts too. I needed a drink and I knew just where to get one. I got in my car and headed up to Wilshire Boulevard. Sonny McLean's. I needed some whiskey. Maybe a lot of whiskey and a blood-rare steak sandwich. I still had the twenty five Benjamins in my pant pocket. Only they didn't seem so crisp anymore. Seemed like they'd been round for a while. Seen things. Been places. Maybe that's just me. I didn't care so much for today. Three young lives lost in twenty four hours. Was this justice? I didn't think so. Not enough people stepping up to the plate and taking responsibility. Including these last two. And just this morning I was having a good breakfast at Joe's Main Diner. I should have thought twice about this job. Seemed too easy from the start. Seemed like it wasn't anything from the start.

I dragged my heavy legs into the small building. Cozied up to the bar and lay my fedora down. Double scotch I said to Brian. He didn't say too much. Must've known I wasn't in the mood for talking. The place was quiet. Just us regulars. I was thirsty so I asked for two more and the steak sandwich. The scotch was warm on the way down. I started feeling better already so I figured I'd close up shop for the day. I banged some numbers into my phone and stuck it in my ear.

"Hello," said a smokey voice this time.

"Marlene?" I asked.

"Yes Mr. Carrick. I heard there are two more dead. Doesn't make me feel any better or any worse."

I nodded at my whiskey. "Yeah," I said. "Melodie and her pal Alvarez. She shot both of them."

"I heard that. John told me." I drank some more scotch and stuck another cigarette in my face.

"You were right about her," I said trying to sound comforting, "She killed your son. Pushed him hard when he was in the shower. The coroner will know the exact cause of death. Alvarez was there too, but he wasn't actively involved. If anything he tried in his way to make it right in the end. I thought you should know that."

She didn't say anything for a while and I had run out of words. I took another drink from my tumbler and I wanted to light my cigarette. My belly was warm and already I was starting to feel better about things. About a whole lot of things.

"Thank you Mr. Carrick. Don't feel bad about it. I don't." Her voice was strong. I knew what she meant. I was the patsy. I didn't feel like keeping her money.

"Well Ms. Greenlaub this was only a day's work so I owe you some Benjamins you gave me."

She coughed a little sad cough to clear her throat.

"Keep them Mr. Carrick, you've earned them. Money isn't anything."

"Good day Ms. Greenlaub."

"Chin up Mr. Carrick, people die everyday."

I didn't thank her. As far as I was concerned this was blood money. I finished my third whiskey as the steak came by. Pink and rare. I put my cigarette back in the pack. I thought about the mess I'd left behind. I didn't feel so hungry anymore. Since she was buying I ordered more whiskey. I needed to collect my thoughts. She was right about one thing though. Money ain't nothing.

Brotherly Love

What I like about living in The Big Orange is the number of people. The city has around 4 million lost souls. And when you have that many lost souls bumping into each other, sparks are gonna fly. And when the sparks fly, the knives and the guns come out to play. That means there're a lot of murders in this juicy orange. It keeps a guy like me busy. Last year for instance, 203 lost souls took the boat to the other side. Every forty-something hours another one bites the dust.

There's plenty of work in this seedy little city of mine if you make your living off the dying. Which is what I do. Indirectly. I'm a private investigator for hire. But there hasn't been a lot of work coming around for me lately. In fact, this past week was as dry as the empty bottle of scotch that stood on my kitchen counter.

Seven days of nothing to do but cultivate belly button lint. I was getting bored. Hell, I was even contemplating committing a felony, just to have something to do. Don't get your knickers all in a bunch, I joke, okay.

But, here I was sitting at my kitchen table staring at a day old strudel so tough it was staring me back. I dangled a finger around my coffee cup, the steam still dancing up from its mouth.

I was thinking about the last seven days. I figured a quick back of the napkin run of the numbers meant I'd missed out on about 4 murders.

Not that I always enjoy this line of work, you understand. But somebody's gotta take out the trash. And well, might as well be me. I'm not that good at much else. Ask Pirate, he'll tell you. He was lying there flat out on his side in a square of warm sun that had tossed itself on the kitchen floor. My mobile started vibrating and I picked it up to have a look at it. It was my good friend John Roberts.

"911, what's your emergency?" I asked.

I heard a chuckle on the other line.

"Sorry, wrong number. I was looking for someone who could actually help."

"I've been waiting for your call all week, Johnny Boy, where you been?"

"I've been looking at dead folk mostly. Listen, Anthony, how are you doing?"

"Bored to tears actually, John. You have something for me to alleviate my boredom?"

"Funny you should ask. I'm standing here in De Neve Square Park and I'm looking down at a dead man. Would you care to join me Anthony?"

"Love to, but I have no idea where De Neve Park is."

"You've got one of them fancy new smartphones, right? Find it on a map. You were a detective, right? I mean, we did work together, or am I thinking of somebody else?"

"You must be thinking of a different Anthony Carrick."

"Okay, I'll see you in about, what, fifteen or so? I'll give you a hint 'cos I'm feeling soft. It's in Holmby Hills."

"Right, just down the street from my house."

"If you say so, pal. Listen, the coroner's gonna be here any minute so get down here as quick as you can if you want to take a look at the corpse."

I hung up with a huge grin on my face. I was getting back in the game. Now, I was hoping for a private gig. A private gig pays double the rate that I can get as a contractor with the LAPD. But beggars can't be choosers. Two hundred and fifty a day is better than a kick in the teeth.

I did as John suggested and I searched for De Neve Square Park on my app. It wasn't going to take me more than fifteen minutes or so to get there. But I had a breakfast to finish first. I took a bite of the strudel and it wasn't too bad for a day old. But I wasn't gonna fight with it to get it down into my belly. A swig of coffee helped wash it down and I was ready to greet the day. If not with a grin on my face, at least a bit of pep in my step.

I left my apartment, giving Pirate a scratch behind his tattered ears before I left. It was a fall day and I grabbed my jacket and hat as I left. The morning was cool, and as I got into my LeSabre it was warm, sitting there sunning itself in the parking lot.

Traffic was steady on my way up the hill to De Neve. It was around eight twenty-five when I got there. What should have been a fifteen minute drive had turned into a twenty five minute slog in smog. I parked on North Parkwood Drive and as I got out, I didn't see the coroner's van anywhere. I was grateful for small mercies. I was at the southwest corner of the park, where the sign and main entrance gave its name.

De Neve Square Park is a small park of about 100 feet wide, almost square. Its perimeter is thick with trees except for an opening on the west side. I looked around and found John in the middle of the park on the east side. I walked up to him. His guys had already taped off the whole park as a crime scene. He was talking with lanky Mike Cardigan, one of LAPD's best crime scene techs.

As I drew up on them Mike adjusted his steel framed glasses and grinned at me from his freckled face. He elbowed John.

"Look what the cat brought in," he said.

"That the best you got this morning?" I asked.

"Hey, what can I say, it was supposed to be a day off, but unlike you, John here wanted to bring in one of the best techs. Can't blame him."

"If you're considered one of the best now, boy, they must be scraping the bottom of the barrel."

I grinned at him and he smiled back.

"Good to see you again, Anthony," he said.

"It sure is."

John offered me a coffee.

"It might be cold by now. I've been waiting for you for the last hour."

He chuckled.

"What the hell, I thought I was at a crime scene, not the Laurel and Hardy show."

"Nope," said John, "wrong on both counts, the is the Roberts and Cardigan biopic."

I took a sip of the coffee. It was creamy and sweet, just how I liked it. And warm too.

"Cheers," I said. "I needed this."

"Rough night?" asked Roberts.

"I went a few rounds with a mean Scotsman last night," I said.

"That so," said Roberts.

"Yeah, Johnnie Walker's a mean sonofabitch."

"You're getting soft Carrick," said Cardigan.

"Are we gonna just hang around here in this park spinning yarn, or are you guys actually gonna give me something?" I said.

"Yeah, sure, come on over here and take a look at our victim."

John led us to the closest clump of trees to him. Under the spindly branches lay a man face down in the dirt. There was a detective squatting down next to the body taking notes. The victim's hands were down by his sides, palms facing up and his head was looking off to his right. His legs were out straight with his toes pointing inwards.

He had on a pair of white sneakers and dark blue jeans. His pants weren't on fully. They were slightly bunched up to one side as if someone had tried to put them on after he was dead. On his upper body he was wearing a navy windbreaker. There were no signs of struggle, from what I could see just looking at him from this vantage point.

I walked over to the right side of the body, bending down under branches. I squatted down and took a sip of my coffee. The victim had pale blue eyes that weren't closed and his face was swollen. It was hard to tell if he was once handsome or not. The mask of death will do that to you. Rob you of any dignity. He had a thick mustache. I think they call it a chevron mustache. The kind gay pornstars wore in the seventies.

It was a good looking mustache if that's your thing. Personally, I like to present a naked face to the world each day.

"I'm going to say you found him like this, right?"

John nodded. He was standing down by his feet.

"Yeah, we found him like this. But as you know Anthony, we're often not the first to find victims."

He grinned at me, always the cad.

"Thanks for the homicide 101 lecture," I said. "Who found him and how did he look at that time?"

I got back up and came back over to John, bowing my head, not so much in reverence, but because I didn't want to get smacked in the choppers by errant branches. John turned his head towards the detective still squatting down on the left side of the victim.

"Hey, Glenn."

Glenn looked up and then stood up and came over to us.

"You met my old friend, Anthony Carrick?"

"No, Captain."

"This is Detective Glenn Blackstock."

He reached out his hand eagerly. I took it and gave it a shake. It was tough like overcooked steak. He was a round fellow and on the shorter side. I'd put him at around five eight. He had ginger hair and a gap between his two front teeth as he smiled at me. His eyes were close together and small.

"I've heard a lot about you Anthony," he said. "It's my pleasure."

"Thanks, Glenn, you've got a good gig here with your Captain."

Glenn nodded and then looked back at John.

"Who called this in, you got that down?"

John looked at Glenn's notebook. Glenn couldn't have been older than mid-thirties, if that. Obviously a rising star in the LAPD. I didn't think it'd take the brass long to tarnish his enthusiasm. Glenn flipped back a few pages in his notebook. He was wearing a brown suit that he bought with foresight. I reckon he could grow into it another twenty or so pounds. His blue tie was knotted just below his first button which was undone.

"That was Ms. Naomi Antonucci, Captain. She called it in at 7:37 this morning."

"Did she say how she found him?" I asked.

"She was on her morning jog around the neighborhood when she came into the park to finish up and stretch. Said she saw some sneakers and then when she went to look further she saw it was actually our vic."

"Speaking of vics, what's our guy's name."

"Ray Hope," said Glenn.

"You're shitting me."

"No sir."

Glenn looked puzzled.

"Well, no more ray of hope for our vic, then."

Poor kid, hadn't been around John long enough to pick up on his macabre sense of humor. John chuckled and saw Mike smirking out of the corner of my eye.

"Anthony, put these on, and I'll let you take poke at the guy's wallet."

Mike handed me some latex gloves. I passed my coffee over to John and put on the gloves.

"Terrific, fit me like a glove."

"Groan," said Mike.

It was early still, I was just warming up. Mike passed me a bag that had Ray's wallet in it. I opened it up and took the wallet out. It was expensive looking, probably soft calf or something. I opened it up, it was a bi-fold. There was a thick wad of bills in it.

"How much?" I asked, not looking at Mike.

"Hundred and thirty five," he said.

There were a couple of credit cards inside. An American Express Centurion and a J.P. Morgan Palladium Visa. There was also a debit card and a couple of photos. One was of a young boy, kneeling behind a soccer ball and the young lad was wearing soccer gear. The background was dotted with kids playing soccer. The other was a family portrait. Posed against a painted gray background. I recognized the vic and I assumed the woman was his wife. She might have been attractive once, but not when the picture was taken.

She looked bloated. Either by too much good living or too many pharmaceuticals to keep the skeletons at bay. The young boy in this photo looked like the kid in the first photo with the soccer ball. In this pic he was older and more sullen. Teenagers.

There was also his driver's license, and from the address I figured he didn't live more than several blocks from here.

One other thing I saw tucked in behind the money was a receipt. It was from a local drugstore. Our ray of sunshine had bought a coke, chips and a candy bar as well as a bottle of lube. I closed up the wallet and gave it back to Mike.

"That's it?" I asked.

"Yeah. Nothing else, except lint in his pockets," said Mike.

"No keys?"

John shook his head.

"Might have had a car or he might have walked here. If he had a car it's probably been stolen. But I think that's unlikely. There's a good chunk of cash still in that wallet, and those credit cards. Man, you could buy yourself a helluva good time with that kind of plastic."

"I wouldn't know about that," I said. "What I do know is that I'm buying my credit card company a helluva good time with all the interest I'm paying."

John patted me on the back and handed back my coffee.

"You shouldn't have left without your pension."

I looked at him sideways.

"You know I didn't have much of a choice."

He nodded his head back and forth as if he were sparring with a partner, weighing the options.

"You could've. That's all I'm gonna say."

I wasn't going to get into it with him again. I looked back over at the body.

"So, that's how the vic was found," I said raising my paper cup of coffee towards the victim. "On his front like that?"

"Yup, like I said before," said John.

"How'd he die," I said, sipping my coffee and ignoring John's snarky comment.

"Let me show you."

John walked back up to the body where Glenn had squatted his round-self next to.

"Can we turn him over for Anthony?" asked John, looking at Mike.

"I have everything I need," Mike said.

"Glenn, do us a favor and turn the perp over."

Glenn grabbed the vic by his jeans and his windbreaker and pulled him over towards himself. Ray's head lolled all the way to his right side again. This time I could see his left profile. There was a dark and matted burgundy dent in his skull, just above his left ear. The blood had mostly congealed and Ray's dark brown hair was matted around it.

"What do you figure did that Mike?" I asked.

Mike shrugged and looked down at Ray's face.

"Bottle of Smuckers grape jelly?"

He grinned at me.

"So Ray was out here having a picnic and somehow smeared his face with grape jelly?"

"Okay, seriously. Probably a heavy blunt object."

I looked over at John.

"Seriously? This is your best crime scenes' guy?"

I nodded my head over at Mike.

"That's brilliant, 'cos I was thinking maybe it was marshmallow or maybe even a nerf ball."

"Gentleman, Anthony."

I knew that voice. Like honey on my ears. I was buzzing and my heart was a flower blossoming. I turned to look at the coroner.

"This is why I get up in the morning to grisly scenes like this," I said.

"Can I take him away?" asked Dr. Stratham.

John nodded.

"Sure, we don't need him anymore."

I winked at Emily as she walked by in her overalls, two body men with her, carrying a stretcher. She smiled at me as she looked over her shoulder in my direction.

"Damn, what did you do to earn the favors of that," said John.

"It's all in my winning charm."

Mike rolled over a large rock towards me. It was the size of a softball or grapefruit, but not as smooth or round.

"You taking to soccer now?"

Mike grinned from up in the clouds, his height seemingly growing by the minute.

"Nah, that's your murder weapon. Well, not that one exactly, but one like it, which I have a hunch the perp left here somewhere in the park."

I bent down and picked it up. It had heft. I tossed it in my hand a few times. Something like this would definitely do the trick.

"Yeah, I like this. Means it was a crime of passion. Something heated happened here that got out of control."

John nodded.

"You wondering why a guy would be out here like this by himself this early in the morning?"

"Thought crossed my mind," I said, taking a sip of coffee. "Maybe he was out for a morning jog."

"In jeans?"

I shrugged. I didn't really think he was out here jogging. But I was playing along with John.

"To each his own."

John shook his head.

"No, Anthony. Guys come out here, married men, to suck cock."

I nearly spat out my coffee.

"Jesus, John, I'm trying to drink here."

John laughed out loud. He thought my reaction was extremely funny.

"I'm just saying. That's what guys come out here for. The neighbors will deny it, but you wait. We're gonna get his computer and we're gonna find him on one of these married-guys-seeking-guys-for-quickies sites."

I looked down at my hands. They were still covered with the white gloves, like I was just about to do a prostate exam. I felt seedy, just standing here. The soil stained beneath my feet with God knows what sorts of bodily fluids. The worst of it all being the cheating and lying.

"Well then, we have a slam dunk," I said, regaining my composure. "But I don't see any spent condoms or other garbage around here."

"Did you look in the garbage can when you came in?" asked Mike.

"No," I said, shaking my head.

"Don't bother, nothing in there of note."

"Thing is, Anthony," said John. "These guys live around here for the most part. They're rich, powerful men who need these indiscretions kept discreet, so what comes in with them goes out with them when they leave."

"How do you know about all of this, John. Something you keeping from me about your personal life?"

"Hey now, that's a low blow. No, we've received some anonymous tips on occasion and patrol has been sent out here to check things out."

"Well, you find out who he came out here to meet and you've got your man on the grassy knoll," I said. "Why'd you even bring me along for the ride. Not that I'm not grateful."

"I miss working with you, pal. And besides as the Captain of Homicide, I can spend the allocated consulting funds how I please."

"Well, gosh, I'm forever in your debt."

"Yeah, and that."

"I'd like to speak to the witness who called this in. Ms..."

"Antonucci," said Mike.

"Yeah, her. I'd like to talk to her about it," I said.

"I was hoping you'd say that," said John. "I'll get her info to you and you can probably sit down with her this morning."

I nodded and finished my coffee.

"I'm gonna go and work on a warrant for the vic's computer, then we can go and visit the grieving widow."

"Sounds good to me."

The coroner walked past, after her two body men who were carrying Ray on the stretcher.

"Don't be stranger," she said to me.

"I won't."

I watched her walk back to the coroner's van and then get into her Prius. I felt weak at the knees. Even in overalls she looked smoking.

"Glenn," said John.

Glenn looked up at his Captain.

"Get Anthony the witness's details," he said.

Glenn wrote some information on a piece of paper at the back of his notebook. He tore it off and handed it to me. I looked at it. It said, "Naomi Antonucci, 505 Parkwood Drive. 310-555-9332."

I was parked on North Parkwood Drive, and it wasn't long enough to have a 500 block, or so I figured.

"Where is this place, Glenn?"

"Well, this here is North Parkwood Drive," he said to me, pointing behind me where my car was parked.

"Yeah," I said, "I parked there."

"Right, but it kinda zags left up there by North Mapleton and then heads north again. I figure the house is up at the end up there."

Now he was pointing past where Ray had not five minutes before been lying, stone cold dead. I didn't think Glenn was the finest traffic cop but I had an idea where he was sending me.

"I think I'll drive," I said, mostly to myself.

"You're getting soft Anthony. A walk will do you good."

"Nope, I don't think so. Marlboros and walking don't go together so well."

I popped open the lid from my finished coffee and took off my gloves. I bunched them into the coffee mug and then put the lid back on. John was on the phone, cops were milling around amongst a few crime scenes guys.

"Mike, we've got something here," said one of his guys. He walked off to check it out. I fished out my phone and dialed Naomi's number. An Hispanic woman, sounding older, maybe in her sixties answered.

"Can I speak with Naomi Antonucci?"

"Yes, who is it?"

"My name's Anthony Carrick, I'm with the Los Angeles Police Department."

"One moment, please."

I didn't have to wait long. In the meantime I watched Mike head over to his guy and they had a huddle around a rock. Like the one he was kicking over to me earlier. Mike nodded, I couldn't hear them. His guy put it in a big plastic bag. That must be the weapon of opportunity I figured.

"Hello?"

"This Naomi?"

"Yes, it is."

"Hi, Naomi, Anthony Carrick,here. I'm with the LAPD and I'm just here at De Neve Park. I'd like to come and speak with you about the victim you called in earlier this morning."

"Okay."

She sounded like she wasn't sure. Like if she had a choice, she'd rather have said no.

"How about in five minutes?"

"Okay."

"Good, I'll see you then."

I hung up the phone and looked around. This was one hell of an opulent neighborhood. I thought something like this would likely ruffle folks' feathers around here. The big orange was moldy in places, but folks like these didn't like to look under the seams. That bright shiny sheen was what they liked to live in. Like a bubble that was gonna slowly burst and everyone was going to get gum on their face.

John was just getting off the phone. I walked up to him.

"I've gotta get going. Another homicide from last night just came in. I'll catch up with you later," he said.

"Sure will."

I walked back to my car and tossed my coffee cup into the trash on my way out of the park. I got in and drove to the address I had already memorized. I parked outside the gates and had to get out of my car to reach the buzzer. Nobody spoke to me, but the gates opened up and I drove in. Must have been my winning charm again.

I walked up to the main doors and just as I knocked, the old Hispanic woman answered. She was wearing a one piece pale blue dress with apron that came down below her knees. She was stocky and short with black hair. That was about the only thing that wasn't natural. She smiled at me.

"Detective Carrick," she said. "Please, come this way."

I didn't correct her but I did follow her into a large living room where a woman sat on a large, hard-looking couch. She had on blue yoga pants and a tight white yoga top. Over that she wore a blue jacket, but it was mostly undone. Her bosom was not a gift from the gods, but manmade. But bespoke, you could tell, not like the ladies down on Ventura Boulevard.

She got up and walked over to me. She was slender and graceful like a dancer but not a professional dancer, maybe more like one whose dance partner is a pole. Though I bet she'd left that a long time ago. She held out her hand. Delicate fingers with a French manicure.

"Detective," she said.

"Please, call me Anthony. You must be Ms. Antonucci?"

"Mrs. but you can call me Naomi. Would you like something to drink?"

Her hand was warm and soft in mine and it disappeared in my mitt like an easy flyball.

"Water would be great."

She nodded at the old lady who had invited me in and she disappeared.

"Please sit, Anthony."

I sat and took off my fedora, placing it next to me. She sat across from me and picked up her bottle of Perrier. The Hispanic lady came back in and handed me my own green bottle.

"Thanks," I said.

"Thank you, Maria," said Naomi. Her voice cool as the bottle in my hands as it started to sweat.

Maria left and I looked over at Naomi. The house was big. I felt small in it. It had no personality. Even the cancer ward was warmer and friendlier than this place. I opened my bottle and took a swig. The fizz bit the back of my throat. I coughed and she smiled at me.

"What happened to Ray?" she asked.

"You knew him?"

She nodded.

"We're reasonably close here as a community. Ray owned a series of high end car dealerships. In fact he got me a great deal on my Cayenne."

"That's nice," I said, trying to feign interest and enthusiasm.

Naomi looked to her right and out the window into an expansive yard, smoother than a putting green.

"So, what happened to him?" she asked again.

I figured I need to rock her world a little bit to get somewhere with her.

"Well, that's what we're trying to figure out. But can you think of any reason why someone would want to beat him to death with a rock."

She looked back at me then, and a wave of horror crawled up and down her like fire ants. But she controlled it pretty quickly. She shook her head.

"That's awful," she said. "Ray seemed like such a nice guy. I can't imagine anyone doing that to him."

"Do you know why he might be out in the park late at night?"

That question wobbled her center again, but she steadied herself. She took a sip of water from her expensive bottle.

"No, that seems strange."

She didn't look at me when she said it. And the way she said it I knew that she knew what went on in that park at night.

"Can you tell me anything else about Ray?"

"Like what?"

"Well, tell me about his family."

"We're not that close. We're close as a community, doesn't mean that we hang out with each other all the time."

"Seems like some of the men do," I thought to myself.

"Ray has a wife and a son. His son still lives with them, he's going to UCLA but I forget what he's studying. His wife's older than me. We don't really hang out at the same places."

"Do you have any problems in this community much, Mrs. Antonucci?"

"No, Mr. Carrick, that's why we live here. With wealth comes some distance from the, um..."

She was looking for just the right word to use. I didn't think she wanted to insult me and she knew I was a working stiff.

"Distance from the struggles that life can sometimes throw your way."

I smiled at her and took a sip of water. It bit me in the back of the throat again.

"You should run for office."

"I rather prefer anonymity," she said.

"Do you know where Ray used to live?" I asked.

She nodded.

"The Hopes live across the road and two houses down. You can't miss it, it has a tennis court right up against the edge of the property."

"Just before I go; you said you'd been coming back from your run this morning when you found him. Is that right?"

"Yes, I'll sometimes stop in the park to do some stretching before I walk the rest of the way. And that's when I saw him. Well, I saw his feet sticking out and I went to investigate. There he was, poor man, face down in the dirt."

"So he was on his stomach?"

"Yes, just like I told 911 when I called it in. Why are you asking me these same questions? This whole experience has been quite upsetting."

"Because I enjoy your company."

She smiled at me. The only real warmth I'd felt in that home the whole visit.

"How was his body positioned?" I asked.

She looked up at the ceiling trying to recall.

"I don't know. He was lying on his stomach, his legs were straight out and his arms were by his side."

"Which way was his face looking?"

She blew air up towards her bangs.

"I don't know. I don't remember. He was dead and I got scared and ran home and then called 911."

"Did you notice any injuries or blood?"

She shook her head.

"Was he messy, dirty, or did he look reasonably clean."

"I don't remember. I think he was clean."

"Was he dressed?"

"Mr. Carrick, what are you inferring?"

"You know what I'm inferring, Naomi. Some of the men in this neighborhood like to meet out at that park, sometimes late at night for, what would you call it?"

I looked at her and waited a moment. Her gaze fell to the floor.

"Brotherly love. Does that sound about right?"

She didn't say anything for a while and then she looked up at me.

"You know, it's easy for you to come in here with your cavalier attitude and smart remarks, but you don't know what it's like."

"I know what it's like to live lies. Ask my ex about it."

"No, you don't. Not really. Sometimes you have to turn a blind eye to get by."

"So the other one can get plucked out, too?"

I leaned in towards her. My elbows on my knees. I was dangling the Perrier in my hand like it was noosed up.

"Listen, Naomi. I don't care what a man chooses to do with another man, or a woman or the both of them. So long as nobody's getting hurt and everything's on the table. I couldn't give a nickel for every dime that asked. But rich people, they hide themselves away from the rest of us because they think they're better than us. But really, you're worse, you sully yourselves with the dirty ends of toilet paper morality and you think you're self-made. You're not self-made, you're made on the backs of the poor. And that really dents my Buick."

I looked at her, trying to see how that washed over her. She didn't seem to mind. She was either used to blunting her feelings or she was using pharmaceuticals for them.

"You know, you'd be welcome here anytime with your tough guy attitude. I find it very exciting."

She got up from her couch and came and sat next to me. She put her hand on my hand.

"What would your husband think?"

"He wouldn't know," she said. "He does what he does and I do what I do."

"You do who you want to do."

She smiled. I wanted to slap some sense into her, but I knew that'd only sting my palm. I stood up, reaching for my fedora.

"When is your husband going to be home?"

She sat there on the couch I had just left, clutching her hands together. She was an attractive woman, no doubt. But I had a feeling she knew the insides of too many bedrooms and the stipple of too many ceilings.

"My husband should be home by eight."

"Good, I'd like to come by for a visit."

She looked up at me then with the faintest frown wrinkling her botoxed forehead.

"You don't play for their team, do you?"

It was a sincere question, but some folks just don't get it.

"I fight for truth, justice and the American way, Naomi. There's been a homicide in your neighborhood. Your neighbor's dead and you're worried about who I sleep with on cold winter nights."

51

I shook my head and started walking towards the front door. "I'm good, you know."

"At what," I said over my shoulder, as I walked out the door and closed it behind me. The sun was burning up the sky really good now. A fireball scarring the blue canvas. Too bad it couldn't burn up the stink in the rotting Big Orange.

I got in my car and turned around to leave. From my rearview I thought I saw her watching me as I went. Sad, hollow lives that not even money can fill.

I exited the Antonucci's drive and headed south looking for the house with the tennis court visible from the road. It was where she said it was. I pulled up on the side of the road just in front of the gates. I took out my phone and dialed John.

"You lost again?" he said when he answered.

"You could say that. But no, I'm outside Ray Hope's place. Has next of kin been informed."

"Not yet. But seeing as how you're there, could you take one for the team?"

"For double my rates."

"Not in the budget, Anthony. You know that."

"Worth a try."

I hung up the phone and looked through the well-manicured hedge, past the tennis court and at the house. There was an Hispanic man watering some flower beds up by the house. I got out of my car, leaving my fedora riding shotgun. I walked over to the gates and paused by the intercom. It had a camera on it too. I pushed it like it was my play on a Vegas slot.

"Hello."

The voice was a woman's. White I would have guessed and older.

"Is Phyllis there?"

"Who's this?"

"Anthony Carrick with LAPD Homicide."

"This is Phyllis," the voice said.

I looked at the camera and put on my stoic, hardboiled face. The sort of face it seems I'm always wearing.

"I have a personal matter I need to discuss with you, in person."

"Come on in."

There was a side gate that buzzed and I pushed it open. It closed behind me and I walked up the long driveway towards the house. I passed the tennis court and it looked pristine. Like it had never been used. The lawn was immaculate and green. That's not a natural color here in The Big Orange. Not that bright green anyway. The gardener looked over towards me and I nodded at him. He looked back at his watering.

The water was coming out of the hose attachment in a large spray like a shower head, and I kept thinking of elephants. Maybe because the hose was black and reminded me of an elephant's trunk. But more than likely because there were elephants in just about all the rooms in all the houses around here.

I got up to the main door of the house, and what do you know if there wasn't a knocker on it that was of an elephant's face. The trunk curved like a J and I used it to knock a sprightly tune onto the door. Sometimes a funeral dirge starts out sprightly. That was me.

An older woman answered the door. Gravity had made a mess of her. Makeup was thick but carefully done, but her whole body sighed like a deflated balloon towards the floor. Her hair was blonde. Unnaturally blonde and she was plump. Not the bombshell I had just shared a Perrier with across the street. Though to be fair, Phyllis, if this is who answered the door was a good twenty years her senior.

I looked at her with a bright smile. She didn't return mine. An aura of imbued unhappiness emanated from her like old grannys' perfumes. I almost gagged on it. But my smile held tight.

"Detective Carrick?" she said.

"Please, call me Anthony."

"Come in."

I walked in behind her and closed the door. This one wouldn't close itself and Phyllis had started up ahead of me. She led me into a living room that was the gauche brother to Naomi's living room. The furniture and ornate decorations reminded me of Napoleon for some reason. Old and flowery and ornate. Above the fireplace was a large painting. I'd guess it was four by six feet, of Ray and Phyllis. Ray sitting in one of the ornately shaped chairs I saw in this living room. Phyllis standing above him with both her hands on his right shoulder. Not a glimmer of a smile shared between them.

I walked up to the fireplace and studied the signature. It looked like Roger Barratt's work. We'd gone to art school together and he was doing well painting portraits of the rich and those who thought they were famous. Last time I bumped into him at an art show he'd bragged about how he'd crack a quarter of a million dollars that year. And that was a few years ago.

I didn't care for him and I didn't care to be prostituting my art for greenbacks.

"Do you like it?" she asked as she came up and stood beside me.

"It's nice," I said, "great technique."

I didn't really want to tell her what I thought of it. I can be an ass, but I needed this woman's help in understanding her husband.

"Please, sit down."

I sat down in an ornate chair. I wanted to call it a French arm chair, but I don't know my arm chairs from my cushions. But that'll give you an idea. The arms on the chair were padded with a floral pattern and they ended in balled fists, in natural wood. It was surprisingly comfortable for such an ornate but rigid chair.

"Can I get you anything to drink."

I shook my head. With the coffee I'd had at home, the coffee John had given me, and the Perrier, I felt like my teeth were bobbing buoys in the back of my mouth. Phyllis came and sat down across from me on a couch that was just a larger version of my chair.

"You are Phyllis, I presume?"

She hadn't given me the courtesy of an introduction so I took one for myself.

"Yes, I thought you knew when I answered the outdoor buzzer."

I smiled. In the corner of my eye I saw movement. A tall lanky young man came into the living room. From the pictures I'd seen, this was the sullen son. I stood up walked over to him and offered my hand. I wanted to see just how sullen he was. He didn't accept it. His hands were thrust deep in his pockets. He was a few inches taller than me, but he'd been in my fighting class. Light Heavyweight, if you were wondering.

He had deep blue eyes and a straight nose. He was a handsome lad if you could get past the sullenness of his features. His hair was a brown, dirty bird's nest of a mess. His mouth was thin and sharp like a shark's and he held my gaze steadily. Then he turned to his mother.

"Who is this?"

He asked in the vacant tone of schoolboy kicking over a dead bird.

"That's Detective Carrick with the LAPD. He has some information about your father."

"Did you look at his badge?"

"Well...no."

Still standing rigidly with hands stuffed in his pocket he looked back at me.

"Can I see some ID?"

I pulled out my PI's license and held it open in front of him. He went to reach for it with his left hand.

"You got eyes on your fingers?"

He stopped for a minute trying to figure out what I meant and then he pulled his hand away and looked at it steadily for a minute until I put it away. He turned back to look at his mother.

"He's not even a real cop. His a private investigator."

He said those last words like he was accusing me of being the whore of Babylon. I wasn't going to let her say anything before she'd heard me out.

"I'm here in an official capacity with the LAPD. I'd suggest you might want to hear what I have to say, Phyllis."

He looked at her and glared. She nodded at me. I sat back down on my French chair, feeling like royalty.

"Please, tell me why you're here."

"I first need to determine that you're both kin of Ray's. I understand you are his wife, Ms. Hope..."

"Ms. Rivera."

"Ms. Rivera, and you are his son?"

I looked at him and he nodded then he went and sat down next to his mother. He kept a steely gaze on me the whole time.

"What's your name?"

"Curtis."

"Curtis Hope or Curtis Rivera?"

"Hope."

I looked back at Phyllis and weighed my words carefully.

"I'm afraid, Ms. Rivera, that we found Ray in De Neve Park this morning. It looks like he's been murdered."

She swallowed hard and blinked her eyes several times. They got wet but they didn't leak. I looked at Curtis. He was looking off someplace in the carpet, chewing his left fingernails. His stare was vacant.

"Murdered, are you sure?" asked Phyllis.

"Yes, ma'am, we're quite sure. You'll be invited to come down to the coroner's office later today, maybe tomorrow, to identify the body, but that's just routine. We know it's your husband we found. ID and photographs found on his body confirm it."

She nodded again and then her wet eyes started to leak. Curtis got up from the couch and disappeared. He came back moments later with a box of tissues and offered them to his mother. She took one and dabbed at her eyes.

"How was he killed?" asked Curtis.

"We can't release that information just at the moment. But it appears, if this is of any comfort, that death was quick and painless."

I don't know why I said that. The two of them, especially the son, didn't seem to be all that concerned. This is the rot behind these gilded walls. The families that put their best faces forward are often wearing masks to hide the monsters underneath.

"Were you close to your father, Curtis?"

He shook his head, took his fingers out of his mouth and looked at his manicuring like a thoughtful professional.

"No."

"Why would anyone want to hurt Ray?" said Phyllis.

Sometimes folks say things because they think they're the right things to say. This family wasn't all torn up about their patriarch's death. They were just putting their best faces forward for my benefit.

"Well," I said, playing along with this ball of yarn as we batted it around like kittens, "if we can determine why Ray was at the park so late at night, we might find motive, and from motive we can often find the killer."

I looked at Curtis and a wave of anger spilled like high tide behind his eyes, but no sooner had I seen it, did it retreat again.

"You said he was at the park late at night?" asked Phyllis

I nodded.

"We haven't confirmed time of death but from all accounts it was after midnight."

"And he was only found this morning?"

I nodded again. Phyllis was getting good at asking the questions and I wanted to get her good at answering them.

"A neighbor found Ray in the park this morning just after seven thirty."

Phyllis dabbed at her eyes again.

"He was all alone all night."

She said it quietly, mouthing the words, feeling them in her mouth like small marbles. She balled up her tissue in her fist and looked out the window to her left, past her son. I didn't know much about this murder yet, but I knew she had some feelings for him. Maybe some distant ones that the sun of misunderstandings and broken dreams hadn't burnt up like morning fog.

"Why do you think he might have been out in the park late at night, Ms. Rivera?"

She turned back and looked at me and tried to put on a brave smile. It didn't look natural on her face.

"You know, Mr. Carrick," she said, her voice broken and sad like a threadbare rug, "about sixty years ago, or more, Elvis Presley used to come out to De Neve Park and play touch football with his friends, when he used to live out here in LA. Simpler times then, I suppose. More carefree and more honest, too, I guess."

She looked back out the window, a wistful far-away look on her face.

"I don't know about that. I think there're some carefree, honest times around now, just not for all folks. You have to practice honesty to get good at it."

She didn't say anything but I thought I saw a smile inch up the corner of her mouth like a worm.

"You know why he was there at the park late at night, don't you?" I asked.

She nodded, at least it looked like a nod. Maybe it was a twitch.

"He was meeting men to have sex. Correct?"

"That's bullshit, that's a fucking lie! My father wasn't a faggot, you can't say that!"

I looked over at Curtis, and he was balling his fists in anger. His face flushed red with it.

"I didn't say he was a faggot, son, but I reckon he was a closet homosexual."

Yeah, I was poking the bear. But the son was either in denial or playing me for a patsy. No way his mother knew without him knowing, too.

"Tell him it's not true. Tell him to stop lying!"

Curtis was almost getting hysterical. His voice was raised and the veins on his neck sticking out like snakes. Spittle was doing squats between his lips. Phyllis reached out and placed her left hand, which still held the balled up tissue, onto his leg.

"It is true, Curtis, you know that. It's okay."

Curtis gritted his teeth and his jaw bulged at the sides like he'd stuffed gum there. But he didn't say anything.

"Still, it doesn't mean he deserved to die. The world needs more love, Mr. Carrick."

"I don't figure how disloyalty and philandering is love, Ms. Rivera, but I'll give you that he didn't deserve to die."

"How can you be so goddamn understanding, after everything that asshole put you through."

Curtis was looking at his mother. Anger still hot on his face like a birthmark. His blue eyes smoldering.

"A part of me still loved him, Curtis."

"No, no. You just couldn't leave because he wouldn't give you a dime, you..."

Curtis found himself finally; he remembered I was in the room. He looked over at me guiltily and saw I was listening, so he looked away and stopped talking. Probably the best for him.

"I did love him, Mr. Carrick, though it was an unrequited love that died a lonely death. But I never gave up on hoping I might become what he needed. Everything that he needed. Can you understand that?"

I nodded. I could understand it. The same way I see the same old suckers at the horse races, their jackets threadbare, the lines of misery written deeply all over their faces, and yet, they still hope their pony will come in one final time, just like in the good old days when they danced with lady luck. Ain't gonna happen.

My phone rang and I answered it. It was John. He asked where I was and I told him.

"Great, can you hang tight for fifteen to thirty? My guys'll be coming by with a warrant and we want to nab Ray's computer before anyone takes wind of it and has a chance to erase it."

"Sure thing, boss," I said, facetiously.

"See, just like the old days."

"In the old days," I said, "I was the boss."

"But this is the new reality. Listen, I also heard back from the coroner. Ray was killed with a hit to the head by that rock Mike found. Coroner also puts his death at between twelve and two a.m."

We hung up and I put my phone away. Phyllis looked at me with a question on her face. I was feeling magnanimous.

"That was the Homicide Captain," I said. "He's heard back from the coroner and your husband was killed by blunt force trauma to the head, sometime between midnight and two a.m."

I already had a good idea who the killer was and he was sitting in front of me. Nine times out of ten the perp and victim know each other. Most times intimately. Phyllis wasn't up to it. I didn't see her heading over to the park after midnight just to confront her philandering husband and knock him on the head with a rock. She'd been living with his disappointment for years.

The son however, I reckon he could be good for it. Just out of his teens, I'd put him in his very early twenties. He's got a huge chip on his shoulder, that I noticed the moment he came into the room. And he's trying to pretend he doesn't know what type of man his father is. I figure, he confronted his father and the whole thing went sideways on him.

But I needed evidence. Well, not me so much as the LAPD Homicide Unit needed evidence. I'm sure they'd get it. There'd be DNA on the rock if they could get at it. And footprints, too. I saw one of the techs taking footprint casts.

Anyway, I wasn't about to tip my hat, I'd left it in the car, and I wanted to find out who Ray's hope was. The man in the shadows with his pants down. Could be a jilted lover or we could have one of those homosexual serial killers out there who prey on closeted men. I'd seen that before. Those homophobes get a real hard on for "teaching" closet homosexuals a lesson.

I didn't have much else to ask. Not until after John and I had figured out who the other man in this cloaked closet was. Then we'd come back and I could ask Curtis some more questions. Even if he wasn't good for this, his alibi was going to be shit. Probably home asleep. That's likely what he'll say. But I had some time to kill, so I asked her if I could get a coffee. I used the washroom too. Just as ornate as the living room.

And we sat and I complimented her on her decoration which got her talking. We spoke about the painter, Roger Barratt and I ended up apologizing for her loss. It was a loss for her. Because even though Ray might have been an ass, she seemed like a sweet woman, lost in a dark night where her youthful dreams had turned to nightmares.

By the time I had finished my coffee, the cops were here with the warrant. I left discreetly and went back home to my apartment the size of Ray's living room. I was working on another painting. This one I was calling Blood Orange. It was about LA. You might have figured it out.

At three thirty I was at the North Hollywood station where John likes to hang his hat most days. I was waiting while the desk cop called John out for me. I knew the routine. I signed in and I was issued a visitor pass. John met me in the lobby. He came up to me grinning and patted me on the shoulder.

"Cat got a mouse?" I asked.

"Yeah, we've got great news, come along and I'll show you."

I followed him through some doors and down some halls. He showed me into a bigger office than the closet we'd met in many times before.

"You're moving up in the ranks," I said. "They've let you out of the closet."

He grinned at me and pulled me a chair to his side. We both sat down.

"I don't have a permanent office here, I grab what I can get. Since you left, we left Parker Center."

"I know. I've seen the new building. Fancy pants. So, when I leave, the department starts finding all sorts of money."

"What can I say. You were too expensive for us to funnel funds anywhere else."

"Right, when I left, Captains didn't get more than a hundred and twenty k a year. Max. That's not enough to make a man rich."

"Well, we do a bit better than that now. I think it maxes at 180, but I haven't got there yet."

"That's all right, but you've put in how many years? Twenty?"

"Twenty five next year."

"Twenty five years to make what a lawyer in this city makes after his first couple of years. And you have just as much of an education."

John grinned at me and shook his head.

"Why do you carry such a hard on still for the department. You and I both came in to serve and protect. It was never about the money."

"You know why, John. I ended up being the patsy. The fall guy. It still poisons my blood."

"I get it, Anthony, I do. But man, that was ten years ago, now. Things have changed in the department. Brass is much better."

"Thirteen years ago now."

"Still, you've gotta let it go. It's gonna eat you up, man."

"You're right."

"And seriously, I've spoken to folks at head office, they'd take you back in a heartbeat."

"What, so I can start as a cadet again, at my age. I don't think so."

"Nah, they'd fast track you. After your eighteen months probationary they'd put you up to detective with a quick route to lieutenant."

I shook my head sadly. I had ten years on the job. If they counted that, I'd need to work a minimum ten years more. Most likely as a detective or lieutenant. It's hard to slide back down the hill you just struggled climbing up for years.

"I'll ponder it. Thanks for looking out for me. You've been a good pal, John. Anyway, what do we have here with the homicide in the park?"

John turned on the computer at the desk and we waited while it booted up and he signed on.

"The computer techs have found a ton of info on Ray the philanderer. He's been active in a gay forum for some time where he's been meeting some men. Let me just get the information up here so I don't mess it up."

I waited and watched as the computer came to life. John opened up his mail and then an email from one of the computer techs.

"Yeah, here it is. Says Ray was a long time visitor to a site called 'gay for a day dot com'. Let's check it out."

"I'd rather not."

"It's not gay porn, Anthony, it's a membership site where guys can meet discreetly."

"What, you a member?"

"Fuck off. But I'm not as homophobic as you are."

"I'm not homophobic."

"Then relax about it and stop getting your boxers in a pinch."

"I don't care what other people do with who they do it to, I just don't wanna be involved."

"Geez, Anthony, seriously, it's not a bug you can catch. Ah, here it is."

The gay for a day site came up. It was very well designed. Not a smack right in the chops, but you definitely knew just by the homepage why you were here. It advertised totally anonymous, discreet hookups for men who had 'other' commitments.

"Do you want to take a tour?"

"No."

John slapped me on the side of the shoulder.

"Just teasing with you, pal. But here's where it gets interesting. When Ray first got on the site he met up with a few guys, but for the last six months, from what we can tell he's been exclusive."

"Is that what we call it now, dickering around behind your wife's back is being exclusive."

John ignored my snarky comments. He was good that way.

"Just listen. This is where it gets interesting. He's been seeing one guy exclusively for about six months now. Okay, cheating on his wife with just this one guy. Happy?"

"I'd be happier if you told me who it was."

John had turned to face me. He looked over his left shoulder back at the computer screen.

"A neighbor. You might have met his wife earlier. The guy is John Antonucci."

I frowned.

"You're shitting me."

John shook his head.

"No, and the kicker is, they had an arrangement to meet at De Neve at midnight last night. I really want to talk to him."

"So do I. When do we leave?"

"Right now if you want."

I nodded.

"I'm still waiting to hear back from Crime Scenes about the shoe impressions they took and to see if they can get any DNA from the rock. They should have something to me by the end of the day."

John logged out of the computer and stood up with me. I pushed the chair back to the far corner of his office. And when I say far, I'm talking a few feet. I walked out of the office after him. We headed out into the parking lot and got into John's unmarked police car.

"Where does Antonucci work?" I asked.

"He works on the fifty third floor of the US Bank Tower. He's a partner at a hedge fund called Night's Son."

John started up the car and we headed out onto Burbank Boulevard. Traffic was getting heavy. John decided on the scenic route which was the 134 East to the I-5 South and then back into downtown on the 110 South. It was forty minutes before we were getting anywhere near the place.

"What do you think about this guy, Anthony?"

"I think he's an asshole. Why these guys can't just own who they are and live honestly is beyond me."

"That's not what I'm asking, smart ass."

John had both hands on the steering wheel. His eyes were front, but he had a grin on his face. I used to love being on patrol with him. We had great times, bantering back and forth.

"I don't think he'll be good for it, John."

John looked over at me for a brief moment before looking back out ahead at the traffic.

"Really? You haven't even met the guy."

"I'm not saying he couldn't do it. Hell, I might give you that he did do it. I'm just thinking he didn't."

"How's that?"

"Well, I met the grieving widow earlier. Well, she was actually a little upset, I'll give her that. I think somewhere deep in her heart she still held a flame for Ray. But I happened to meet the son, too. Real wound up type. Tighter than Mayweather's cross. He's got a chip on his shoulder the size of Nebraska and the temperament to lose his cool in a flash."

"Yeah, but you haven't met Antonucci yet."

"True, so we'll see how it goes. But why kill your lover you've been involved with for the last six months. Unless there were some arguments that you haven't told me about, yet?"

I looked over at John.

"You holding out on me?"

"No. Didn't see anything in their conversations that would indicate animosity. But they were also pretty cagey in messaging back and forth. Just kept it to the basics of when and where. They didn't personally email each other either, so the only interesting conversations probably happened in person or maybe over the phone. Neither of which are recorded."

"Well, let's see how our meeting goes then with Antonucci. But I gotta tell you John, I'm liking this kid for it."

"He's that young?"

John pulled up into a parking spot on West 5th Street, and turned off the ignition.

"I'd say he's about twenty, twenty one, somewhere in there. About six two or thereabouts. Lanky with it. How tall was the vic?"

"Around five ten I think the coroner said."

"So this kid, Curtis is his name, is more than capable. I'd guess, if he did it, it went something like this. He went to confront his father in the park. He'd probably had enough of it. Seen how it had affected his mother and he wanted to get his old man to do the right thing. But he sees his father with another man, maybe it sets him off and he waits until the other man has left and then he just bashes his father's head in."

John nodded his head from side to side.

"You spin a good yarn," he said.

"Could happen."

"Sure it could. But so could Antonucci have done it. Let's go and see what he has to say."

We got out of the car and jogged across the street to the main entrance of the Bank Tower. We took an elevator to the fifty-third floor. It opened up to a large reception area. A pretty blonde was sitting behind a high desk. She smiled a bright smile, as white as paint chips.

"Good afternoon, gentlemen," she said.

I already felt appreciated. A gentleman in a fedora. Not sure about John though. John pulled out his badge and opened it up for her to see. Her smile didn't waver.

"Captain Roberts with Homicide," he said, all business voice. "I'd like to see John Antonucci."

She spoke to him through a smile.

"I'm afraid Mr. Antonucci is in a very important meeting. If you leave your card, I'll be sure he gets it."

John looked at me and it was my turn to grin.

"Listen, doll," I said. "You look like you're trying to do the right thing. But believe me, you know how many blonde bombshells have tried to keep the gate closed to me? Lots, and none of them have been successful. I look at dead people for a living and we'd like to speak with Mr. Antonucci. We can do it one of two ways. You can take the better road and call him out of his meeting, real discreet-like. He'll thank you for that once we're gone. Or, behind door number two, me and my pal here, and he's the bad cop, are gonna go walking all around here, with loud noises and badges flashing looking for Mr. Atonucci ourselves. And when we find him, we're gonna haul him out by his ear. So which door are you gonna choose, darling?"

She pinched her lips and took her eyes off me. Her smile was long gone, mine was just growing. She picked up the phone and tapped at some numbers.

"There are two homicide detectives here to see you, Mr. Antonucci. They say it's very important."

She listened for a bit and then put the receiver down.

"He'll be right out."

"You did the right thing," I said to her.

John and I stood leaning on her desk, while she tried her best to ignore us and get back to her typing. She answered the phone once, too, while we waited. After a minute or two an impeccably dressed man walked into the reception area through frosted glass doors. He looked around quickly, but there was no one else in the reception area except us and the receptionist. He came up to us.

"Mr. Antonucci?" asked John.

He nodded.

"I'm in a very important meeting, I would have preferred to see you later."

"And we'd prefer people didn't go around killing each other," I said.

"You can make this quick and easy if you'd like, or slow and painful," said John.

Antonucci was of average height, slim but with a small soft belly under his tailor-made navy pinstriped suit. He wore a red tie over a white shirt and his arms were crossed over his chest. He wasn't much to look at. You'd probably not notice him in a crowd. To me he looked like a less handsome Patrick Stewart with the same hairstyle. He was clean shaven.

"Okay," he said. "Come with me."

We followed him through the frosted glass doors and turned right down the hallway. We traveled to the far corner of the floor where he led us into his office. His office was the size of my apartment. So it seemed. It looked west out over Maguire Gardens. He closed the solid wooden door behind us and came and sat down behind his dark wooden desk.

John and I sat down across from him. The view was terrific. The day was warm and bright.

"Okay," he said. "How can I help you detectives?"

"It's Captain," said John.

"Captain," said Antonucci, tightly.

"You know why we're here," said Roberts.

"Actually, Captain, I have no idea why you're here, other than I find the intrusion of the LAPD to be rude and impudent."

Antonucci was leaning in on his desk, looking at each of us in turn. I thought he was playing it straight.

"Let's start off with a soft ball," I said. "Where were you between midnight and two a.m. last night?"

He leaned back into his chair, and looked away from me before replying.

"I was at home in bed with my wife."

"You really want to play it slow and painful, Mr. Antonucci?" I asked. "I met with your wife this morning. She had some different things to say."

He started to look hot under the collar. He swallowed and breathed deeply.

"For god's sake, just tell me what this is about?"

"It's about Ray Hope," said John.

"Jesus, is he okay?"

Antonucci gritted his teeth and looked at me.

"No, he's not okay, that's why homicide is visiting you."

"Fuck."

He said it under his breath and then sighed before combing his hands through his hair which only covered the sides of his head.

"Listen, I'm going to make it easier for you," said John. "We know about gay for a day, but what we want is some honesty. Where were you between midnight and two a.m.?"

Antonucci swivelled his soft leather chair to the side and stared out the window. Maybe he was looking towards De Neve, but he didn't have a good view of it from his office.

"I loved him," he said, soft as a mouse running across carpet. "I guess it doesn't matter, anymore."

He turned back around and reached into his pocket and pulled out a handkerchief. He dabbed at his eyes, which had misted up.

"I see the way you look at me. But I don't care. We had something special."

"The world could use a little more love, but lies and deceit. Well, that's a dog's breakfast," I said.

He nodded his head.

"I couldn't come out. The firm would be ruined. The kind of people I deal with, everything's got to be just so. It's all about image and power and façade, Detective."

"Anthony Carrick. You can call me Anthony."

"So yeah, Anthony, it's easy to judge, it's a lot harder to live by ironclad rules of honesty. Maybe in your world."

"Mr. Antonucci, we're not here to judge morality, as much as my friend might like to. But we need to know where you were last night between midnight and two a.m."

He sighed again, looked down at his desk before looking back up at John.

"I guess it's time to start being honest. I was with Ray at De Neve Park. I met him at midnight and I was back home again by 12:45. He was alive when I left. He said he wanted to enjoy the lingering feeling of our time together, under God's night sky. Those were his exact words. His last words to me."

"Can anyone else verify that?" I asked.

He shook his head.

"Nobody except Ray. I slipped out of bed and back in while my wife slept."

Antonucci looked over at John. His eyes still watery, his face the color of spoiled milk.

"What happened to him?"

"He was murdered. Bashed over the head with a blunt, heavy object."

"Oh, God."

Antonucci's lower lip trembled like an autumnal leaf in heavy wind. He dabbed at his eyes again with his handkerchief.

"Who could have done such a thing?"

"That's what we're trying to find out." said John.

"Did Ray give you any indication that someone was out to get him?" I asked.

Antonucci shook his head. He put his arms across his chest again and leaned back into his chair. His desk was immaculate. Not much on it except for a pen and pencil holder a telephone and dual computer screens. A pad of paper was off to one side and a picture of his wife in a bikini was angled, prominent as a trophy, so that guests might see it.

"Nobody that Ray told me about. He was really well liked by the whole community. Most of us had bought cars from him. I got my wife's Cayenne from Ray and he was a pleasure to do business with. The epitome of professionalism. I think that's one of the things that made him so successful. Bespoke high end car sales and service."

"What about his employees?" I asked.

Antonucci looked out the window again, perhaps reminiscing about his last night with his lover over yonder in the square patch of park.

"Not that he ever said anything about any of them. His business was flourishing and because of that, his employees felt secure in their jobs. And anytime I saw any of them interact with him they all seemed really happy. I asked him about it and he said that treating them with respect and paying them decently was all it took to keep them happy."

"And what about you, Mr. Antonucci?" asked John. "Did you have any reason to be unhappy with Ray?"

Antonucci looked back at John and offered a smile as weak as tea.

"I get it. I do. I'm the number one suspect, but Ray and I never said an angry word to each other in the six months we've been together. You probably can't understand this, but we loved each other. We were even considering coming out, to hell with the consequences. Our last night together, was...well, it was wonderful, and I'm glad for that. I'm glad we parted happily."

Antonucci looked down at his lap and balled his handkerchief with a clenched fist. Then he folded it into a rectangle and brought it up to his eyes to dry the salty tears.

"You said that you were considering coming out," I said. "Don't you think family might have known already?"

Antonucci looked at me through wet, red eyes and offered me the same serving of smile he'd offered just moments before to John. He shrugged.

"Maybe they suspected something. But we were really careful. I imagine the only way you found out about us was through the site we messaged through. We didn't leave any traces otherwise. No text messages from our phones, no phone calls from home phones and no emails."

John nodded.

"I'm not stupid enough to believe that my wife didn't know something might be up. I'm sure she suspects an affair of some sort. I mean, I haven't been intimate with my wife for years. And I know for a fact it's the same with Ray. Was the same with Ray."

"I had the impression," I said, "that Phyllis, Ray's wife..."

"I know who she is," Antonucci said.

"I had the impression both she and Curtis knew about Ray's philandering, with other men."

Antonucci nodded.

"Yes, I suppose so. I mean, I found Ray on that site when I joined about eight months ago. If I remember correctly, Ray had joined a few years ago now, so I guess he'd been sneaking out long before I came to terms with who I was."

"Did he mention anything to you about his family being upset, or knowing what he did?" asked John.

"Well, early on we were discussing how to keep everything discreet. In the very beginning of our relationship he had confessed to me that his wife had confronted him about his affairs. He said she'd found his internet bookmarks and the site where we were both on. She'd even managed to read some of his messages to and from others. That was when he had a really easily guessable password. Though I don't know if he ever changed it..."

"No, he didn't," offered John.

"So she was very upset, as you can imagine. And rightly so, I guess. She wanted a divorce but he couldn't risk it. He serves the same kind of people that I do. If word got out that not only was he dickering around behind his wife's back but that he was doing it with other men, he'd be ruined."

"So what did he do?"

"He said no. He said he'd fight her tooth and nail, move all the money offshore and he'd do his best to make sure she got nothing. Phyllis hasn't worked a day in her life and I guess that scared her. But he held out a carrot, too. He said if she'd just bear with him for the next five years, he'd sell his car dealerships and give her half and she could do what she wanted."

"How did she like that idea?"

"He said she begrudgingly accepted it on condition that he not embarrass her. Which I took to mean that he continue to be discreet."

"Anyway the son might have heard about this?" I asked.

"Very likely, he said that it was one of the few times he and Phyllis had a row and Curtis was at home, allegedly sleeping."

John nodded, he was scribbling notes in his pad, had been this whole time. I was only getting paid half my rates, so I figured manual exercise like that was uncalled for.

"But like I said, we were talking seriously of just putting ourselves out there, whatever the consequences. Ray had already started entertaining offers on his business."

"How much was it worth?"

"Ray figured he could get fifteen to twenty million for it."

He threw that number out there like it was an old tennis ball his dog had played with for years. Easy, I guess, for some folks to throw around large numbers like that.

"Our forensics team is working their way through a lot of evidence," said John. "We've got shoe prints, we're collecting DNA from the victim and the murder weapon. Now's the time to come clean while we might be able to put in a good word with the DA."

Antonucci's face got a little paler if it could.

"Listen," he said. "You'll find my shoe prints there, you'll also find, uh...my DNA on Ray, probably, but I swear to you, I didn't kill him. So whatever murder weapon you think you've found, I didn't use."

John looked at him steadily. Antonucci held his gaze for a while before turning his chair and looking outside again. John looked over at me and I nodded at him. We were done here. I had my killer, and his name was Curtis.

"I shouldn't have to say this," said John. "But just to be clear, Mr. Antonucci, stay in town for the next few days while we wrap this up, just in case we have anything else we need from you."

"I'm not going anywhere," he said, looking out the window.

John and I got up from our chairs across from his large desk. I turned around just before leaving.

"You might want to do something with your eyes before you go back to your meeting."

Antonucci looked back over to me. He didn't smile this time.

"I have eyedrops," he said.

John and I left his office and walked past the receptionist on our way out. I grinned at her like a Cheshire cat. She offered a pinched smile that you could bend quarters with.

We were outside waiting for the elevator when John turned to me.

"You're such an ass."

I looked over at him and furrowed my brow.

"What do you mean?"

"Do something with those eyes. Jesus, Anthony, where's your compassion. Clearly the guy is torn up over this."

The elevator door opened up and John walked in. I followed after.

"Sometimes I'm an ass. For sure, I'll take that. But this time John, you've got me pegged wrong. I was just trying to be sincere. Questions are going to be asked if he heads back into his meeting looking like he's been crying. You heard him, his business requires him to be discreet about who he is. That's all. Nothing meant by it."

John and I stared at each other softly for a while, like two bulls between an electric fence. John looked away at the door.

"Okay," he said. "Sorry, I thought you were being an ass."

"All right."

"You know that warrant I got for the Hope's place?"

We were sitting back in John's office in the North Hollywood station. It was after six and I was starting to get hungry. I nodded at him.

"It also included broad access to any other evidence that might be collected. And one of those things was a pair of Curtis' shoes."

I grinned.

"So you're coming round to my side."

He shook his head and smiled at me.

"I figured it had to be someone close to him. A homicide like that, well, it isn't well planned. It's full of passion and spur of the moment. You know that. You don't hardly find riff raff in Holmby Hills much, and a guy out there late at night, you know what he's up to. Especially with a moustache like that. Anyway, I figured it must have been somebody close to the vic, and seeing as we were going to his home, might as well come away with whatever evidence might be kicking around."

"Thanks for the lesson in policing. Tell me about the shoes."

"Right. So they match one of the two print types found at the scene that weren't the vic's. They also match the soil that was there under the trees where the vic was found."

"That's great, but it's not a slam dunk."

John nodded.

"I know, but Curtis probably doesn't know that. I want to take a run at him. I think he might crack. We'll bluff him. Forensics needs more time with the rock to determine the DNA. In the meantime, I figure we might have enough for a DNA warrant. We can play that card with him too."

"I like it. When do we leave, I want this wrapped up because I'm getting hungry and cranky."

"We can leave now. And if he folds like cooked pasta, then dinner's on me," said John.

"With my help, he'll fold like a warm blanket right out of the dryer."

We headed out and got into John's unmarked police car. He decided on the I-10 West and then the I-405 North. It was a thirty minute drive before we pulled up to the Hope/Rivera mansion. John put his arm out the window and pushed the buzzer. Phyllis answered and let us in.

"Let me take the lead on this," said John as we both got out of the car and walked up to the front door.

"I wouldn't have it any other way."

John grabbed the elephant's metal trunk and rapped the door with it. Now that I was looking at it for the second time I noticed how much larger the trunk was considering the elephant head's size. I couldn't help but think it was some sort of subtle phallic symbolism that Ray had planned. Phyllis opened the door.

"Hello again," she said to me.

John introduced himself. She smiled at him. A feeble smile that wobbled and then fell off her face. She invited us in.

"Not to be ungrateful, but I'm getting a little tired of seeing so much of the LAPD today."

We went back into the living room I had sat in earlier this morning. John and I sat together on one of the couches angled at ninety degrees to the couch Phyllis sat on. Our backs were to the windows, and beyond the windows was the lawn and tennis courts.

"How can I help you this evening?" she asked, sighing.

I started to think that maybe Curtis had bailed. That wouldn't look good on him. Wouldn't help his case, but a young hothead might do that. We took his shoes earlier in the day. He's got to realize it's gonna come full circle.

"We'd like to have a word with your son, Curtis," said John. "Is he in?"

Phyllis nodded.

"Yes, I'll go and get him," she said.

"I'm here," he said, walking into the living room from the hallway.

He hadn't changed, hadn't even showered, so it seemed to me. His hair was still messy bird's nest. He wore the same white shirt and blue jeans he had been earlier and he wore a pair of sandals on his feet. Maybe I was getting soft, but in the right light, give him a beard and he could play Jesus at the local production of the passion. Though in truth, his role was probably better suited to Judas.

"Why don't you have a seat, Curtis," said John.

Curtis sat down next to his mother and started chewing away at his nails on his left hand.

"You're left handed?" I asked.

He nodded and kept at chewing his nails.

"Can you tell us where you were last night between midnight and two?" asked John.

"He was here at home asleep," said Phyllis.

"How do you know?" asked John.

"Well, I, er...I was here and I know he was here too."

"You were awake last night between midnight and two?"

Phyllis gave John a long, tired stare, before slowly shaking her head.

"Then I'll ask him again. Where were you between midnight and two?"

Curtis looked past us and out the window. He swallowed before he spoke.

"Asleep in my bed."

He didn't look at us when he answered. He told a pretty good lie, all things considered. I didn't pick up any nervous twitch from him. Just a bald faced lie.

"You really want to do this in front of your mother?" I asked him.

He looked at me. His face as calm as marble.

"Your mother, who you were trying to protect?"

He looked over at his mother for a split moment and then quickly looked away again.

"What's he saying?" Phyllis asked, putting her hand on his knee.

Curtis didn't say anything. He kept chewing away at his nails like he was trying to chew his way out of a leg hold trap.

"You know we took some of your shoes out of the house earlier in the day. And we found a match at the scene. You want us to explain it to your mother or do you want to do the right thing. DNA's coming back from forensics and a DNA warrant is going to be served here pretty soon too," said John.

Phyllis' mouth gaped open. She looked at Curtis who was studying the flora outside the window, just over John's right shoulder.

"Curtis," she said. "What have you done?"

He turned to his mother then and stopped chewing his nails.

"I killed him okay. I fucking killed him. He's never been a father to me, and as for a husband, he treated you like shit."

Phyllis looked down and pinched her lips together, frowning.

"Why did you do it, son?" I asked.

Curtis turned and looked at me.

"Because he was a bastard and a son of a bitch. I didn't plan on it, okay. I was sick to fucking death of the way he treated us. He never had a kind word for me or my mother. Hell, he didn't even give a shit about me. I don't think he even wanted me. But that's not why I did it."

Curtis put his hands to his face and rubbed his eyes. He squeezed them shut and then opened them again. His hands trembled as he tried to find them something to do.

"Look, I went to confront him. I was sick and fucking tired of him fucking all these men and treating my mother like shit. I just wanted him to leave, okay. Leave us the fuck alone. When I walked down there, I passed that fucking neighbor on his way back. And when I got there, my father was pulling up his pants. I was fucking mad. I told him to stop this bullshit, and he told me it was none of my concern and that I should just go home. I told him he was killing my mother and he told me I knew nothing about it, that I was just a sniveling spoilt brat. That's when I lost it. He turned around to do up his pants and I picked up the closest rock and hit him over the head."

"Oh, Curtis, no, no, no," said Phyllis, tears streaming down her face. "Why, oh why, did you do it?"

She was hugging herself tightly and rocking back and forth on the couch. John made a phone call and while we waited for a pickup to come I felt awkward. There was no pride in this for me. I'd sooner people didn't kill each other. Picking up the pieces afterwards made me feel like a trash collector more times than not.

"I'm not sorry I did it," said Curtis. "Now my mother can be free of that asshole, and me, too."

I could understand that. I could see how he felt he was cornered with no way out. Doesn't make it right, though. But parents fuck up their kids like that. Squeeze them 'til the joy and hopeful sap of youth is right out of them. Then you've got nothing left but a hot burnt ember. Like Curtis. I'd seen it before.

I got up and let the two uniforms in and they arrested him and led him out of the house.

"I did it for you, mom. I did it for you," he said looking back at her over his shoulder as they led him out.

But she just kept rocking and hugging herself on that couch. John and I waited until a lady from Social Services showed up to offer some comfort. We let ourselves out then. It was coming up on seven-thirty. I pulled out a cigarette and fired it up. I blew smoke at the darkening sky. John stood next to me for a bit and looked up at the stars starting to twinkle in the sky.

"The Big Orange is starting to peel," I said, looking straight out towards the road.

John grunted and nodded his head.

"But we did good work and I owe you a meal. Your choice."

All In

It was a quiet night in Santa Monica, and the lazy hum from the cars driving by was like the soft kiss of the sea. It ebbed and flowed with the tide of traffic lights always thinking independently and never sequentially in this part of time. I had a paint brush in my hand with a dollop of red paint on the end. Might've been mistaken for a knife with red blood. But I was painting. It was something called "Time's Mistress". I didn't have a clue what it was about, but I was painting like my life depended on it.

And it did. Rent was a week away, and the last painting I'd sold was back when Rembrandt was sitting on his father's lap in knickers. Pirate needed food, and I needed a drink, but the drink could wait until I had the money to pay for it.

It was getting harder to find a decent gig in this town for an ex-homicide detective now working as a PI. Murder and Sons were still on double shifts but folks trusted the cops to figure it out, and that wasn't a bad idea, normally. What most of them didn't realize was that only about one in three murders in this city of sleepy angels gets solved.

Though the movers in shakers in Hollywood and Beverly Hills who could afford a gumshoe like me got better service and higher clearance rates from LAPD's finest.

What I'd been feeding myself with were discreet infidelities. What that really meant was the wife was looking to catch her dandy of a husband but couldn't afford to pay me my regular rates, because you know, he might see the missing money from their joint account.

Now I'm not really complaining, a couple hundred bucks for a day or two's work wasn't nothing. It kept paint on my brush, a cigarette in my mouth and Scotch in my glass, but it wasn't gonna top up my 401(k).

Work had dried up like the antifreeze in my LeSabre last time I'd been out to Death Valley. It had gotten so bad I'd been looking at the help wanted section, and thinking about clipping hedges and mowing lawns. At least speaking English was a plus.

But right now I was lost in my painting, streaking the canvas with red paint that looked more like arterial spray when my cell phone buzzed. I looked at the screen. It was my old pal John Roberts. I picked up the phone.

"Johnny Rotten," I said.

A laugh on the other side.

"You busy tonight, Anthony?" he asked.

"You asking me out on a date?"

More laughing.

"Keep telling yourself that. I've got a guy here who's not saying much. Figure you used to be a murder whisperer."

"Where are you?"

"I'm at the Malamar Hotel down on North Sepulveda Boulevard. You know it?"

"Practically my second home," I said to him, lying.

"Good, then I'll see you in a bit."

I hung up, and already my mood had improved. Not because I'd heard from Captain Roberts, but because there was some money to be had for helping LAPD's boys in blue. I got out of my painting overalls that looked like I'd been in a paintball fight and put on my old detective clothes. Brown slacks and a blue shirt. I grabbed my fedora and headed out to see what the night had dragged in.

I took the Pacific Coast Highway, which at times thinks it's a long dead president before changing it's mind again. The traffic at around two in the morning was quiet. It's about the only good time left to drive down Route 66 nowadays, except the cops are out looking for speeders.

That didn't bother me, I drive slow. I've never mistaken the LeSabre for Ford GT, and Roberts is fed up with canceling my speeding tickets anyhow. Besides, there's no rushing the dead, and driving along the PCH with my windows down and the salty air in my nose reminded me of the good old days. The forties and fifties. When I wasn't even a twinkle in my father's eye.

I arrived at the main parking lot of the Malamar Hotel which was crawling with black and whites and an ambulance which wasn't needed. Sometimes the medics just come out for a look see when their shifts slow. This must've been one of those nights.

The Malamar Hotel is one of those places that thinks putting lipstick on a pig means you can charge for a tenderloin. It ain't so. The place might have been swanky in the seventies. Nowadays under low lights it's pickpocketing tourists and Angelinos who just don't know any better. Not saying it's a bad place. In fact this is the first homicide here I'd heard of. But a couple of coats of paint and an indoor pool that'll gas you with its chlorine stench ain't worth two hundred bucks a night. Not when the hum of traffic is louder than a wasp's nest under your bed.

I donned my fedora and asked one of the young officers where Roberts was. He was on the third floor. I cursed under my breath and headed to room 303 to see what the fuss was about. The Malamar didn't even have an elevator. Classy. Not that I was outta breath when I got there, but I wasn't thinking of my Marlboros either.

As it turned out, 303 was on the far side of the set of stairs I'd chosen. You couldn't miss it. Officers were crawling in and out of the room like termites on driftwood. A smart looking officer whose uniform hadn't seen a scuffle yet didn't let me in.

"Get Roberts," I said. "He'll tell you what to do."

The young fella didn't have the chance. Roberts was crossing the entranceway of the room when he saw me and grinned. He came up to the officer and put his meaty hand on his shoulder and told him I was with them. He moved out of the way to let me in.

"So what have we got?" I asked Roberts.

"A dead body."

"You don't say. So what am I doing here?" I asked.

"You've gotta ask?"

I shrugged at him as we stood facing each other. He put his arm around my shoulder and led me into the living area of the hotel room.

"I heard your last show didn't go so good. Figured you could use a couple of bucks."

"It would've gone better if you'd have bought something, you cheap bastard. You sure you're not Scottish."

He was, but on his mother's side. He told me that as if it didn't count.

"Can't afford your stuff anyway," he said. "Besides, why can't you paint like Norman Rockwell?"

He grinned at me thinking he was funny.

"Why can't you appreciate real art?"

"Okey dokey," he said. "Onto more serious matters. This here is Marsden Hartley."

We were standing within kicking distance of a middle aged man who was lying staring at my shoe. His eyes were open and his mouth slack. It made him look like a guppy. There was a bullet hole in the middle of his forehead which had drooled a small river of blood which was now drying and thick.

Marsden Hartley looked to be in his late forties or early fifties, but he could've been a decade older. His hair was colored jet black and wavy. It was a great head of hair, and even as he lay awkwardly crumpled like a yoga guru on the floor, his hair was immaculate. He was tanned, but you could tell he was careful about it, and probably used moisturizer.

As I looked down at him, I figured I was looking at the godfather of metrosexuals. He had on a pink shirt that was open two buttons too many. He probably would have called it salmon. A puff of gray hair across his chest gave away his age. A chunky gold chain dangled from his neck. He was fit and handsome, though he hadn't been blessed by the Greek gods. He had earned his looks the old fashioned way. From plastic and iron. Cosmetic surgeons and personal trainers. His pants were cream and he wore white deck shoes without socks.

He looked to me like he cost a million bucks. And I had no idea what he was doing in a dump like this. His left hand was palm up by his knee. He had on his ring finger a big piece of silver bling. I grabbed the fleshy part of his hand and turned it up as I kneeled down to take a look.

"Did you see this?" I asked, looking up at Roberts. "It's the New York Giants Super Bowl ring."

Roberts nodded, not looking very impressed.

"I doubt it's real," he said. "You can get those things on eBay for forty bucks."

And he was right. But somehow this one felt different. I pulled it off Marsden's finger. It was heavy and big. It covered pretty much the whole first phalanx of his ring finger. I held it in my hand weighing it in my mind. It must have weighed at least half a pound.

I tossed it over to Roberts and he caught it.

"Pretty heavy," he said.

"Pretty real, I reckon."

"I'll have my guys check it out."

"Can do, or I can tell you who it belongs to."

I grinned at him. He looked at me sideways.

"Is that right?"

"It is."

"Then whose is it?"

"Larry James Baines."

"You're shitting me," he said. "You mean to tell me, that this ring belongs to Larry J. Baines, the wide receiver for the Giants."

"The very same."

"The guy with the most receiving yards ever?"

Roberts was smirking at me now as if I was having him on. I grinned and nodded at him as if I'd just swallowed a mouse.

"I don't believe you."

"Take a look on the inside of the ring's band."

Roberts held the ring up to the ceiling light and took a look at it. Sure enough inside it was inscribed with "Larry J. Baines".

"Well I'll be a monkey's uncle."

"Yes, you are," I said.

"Funny," he replied. "Villacorta!"

A detective who was standing outside the hotel room came back in. He was an average looking swarthy guy. Short brown hair and naturally brown skin. I figured him for Italian or something like that. He wore a brown suit that he'd picked off the rack from JC Penney's. Probably without even trying it on first. He walked up to us, carrying a notebook and pen.

"Captain," he said.

"Have you met my pal, Anthony Carrick?"

Roberts cocked his neck towards me.

"No, I haven't," said Villacorta, as he extended a hairy hand at me and we shook.

"Anthony here was the only detective in LAPD's history to close one hundred percent of his cases."

"Is that right?"

"It is."

Villacorta was now looking impressed. Roberts handed him the ring.

"Log this for me," he said.

Villacorta brought out a small plastic bag from his jacket pocket and put it in. He wrote something on it with his ball point pen and then tucked it back into his pocket. He jotted something else down in his notebook.

"The guy doesn't look like a football player," said Villacorta.

"He's not," I said. "The ring belongs to Larry Baines."

"No shit?"

"No shit," I answered.

"Anthony thinks it's real. I want you to bring in Mr. Baines for an interview and ask him about it."

Villacorta nodded.

"Stick around," said Roberts to him. "We might have some questions for you."

Villacorta nodded again, like he was a bobblehead on the dash of a police cruiser.

"Can we turn him over?" I asked Roberts. He nodded and we turned the vic over.

I took a closer look at his third red eye. There didn't seem to be any burning or gunpowder residue around the entrance wound. I took out my phone and snapped a picture of him. The mask of death wasn't pretty. It never was. Might as well have been looking at a slab of butcher's meat.

"Must have been shot from a couple of feet away," I said.

"That's what we figure," agreed Roberts.

"Who found him?"

"Housekeeping. Neighbor got back from the bar downstairs just after one. Said there was a racket coming from this room."

"A fight?"

"No, blaring TV. He couldn't stand it so he called it in. Housekeeping came up couldn't get the guy to open up, so the manager came up and let them both in. Housekeeping turned down the TV."

I nodded and looked over Marsden. There didn't seem to be any sign of struggle. The room was neat and tidy. It was a nice room for a dive. A sofa against the far wall where Marsden was probably sitting when he was shot. A coffee table with nothing on it just to his side. The bed was on the opposite side of the room. A TV stood on a chest of drawers with a swiveled base. Next to the chest of drawers was the bar fridge. I walked over to it and opened it up. It was fully stocked.

The queen sized bed had two bedside tables. On each was a plastic cup and in an ice bucket was slushy ice with a half full bottle of cheap champagne. It was sparkling wine, the grapes had likely never heard of France. It was a bottle of Gruet Brut. An American attempt at champagne. A good one too, at least for ten bucks.

The bed was the only thing that was messed up. It wanted to tell me its dark secrets but I didn't want to hear about it. I walked to the far side of the bed by the window and looked out over the parking lot. Like I said, this was a swanky place. The windows were closed and the hum of the traffic was an annoying mosquito in your ear. I looked at the bedside table. This side's plastic cup had a smear of pink lipstick. I started to get the idea.

"What did you find in his pockets?" I asked Roberts.

"Just his wallet. His car keys were on the bedside table."

"What did he drive?"

"A 2005 M5."

"What was in his wallet?"

"Driver's license and wad of cash. Almost a grand."

I turned and walked back over to Roberts.

"Anything else?"

"A picture of him with his wife. At least that's what we figure. We're gonna look into it. He also had a fifty dollar chip from Rustler Casino."

"Larry's emporium of debauchery."

"It's just a casino," said Roberts.

I walked into the bathroom and the sink was filled with male grooming products, expensive cologne. A crumpled and damp bath mat was just outside the shower and towel had been thrown casually against the wall by the toilet. I glanced into the trash can. A white slimy slug of a scumbag was lying dead on top of facial tissue. Nice. I walked back out.

"There's a scumbag in the trashcan for your guys," I said to Roberts.

"A what?"

"Condom."

"I see," said Roberts. "And where do you come up with this stuff?"

"MTV mostly."

He laughed.

"I'll get crime scenes on it."

"You mean Cardigan?"

"Yeah, he'd love that. Sadly he's not working tonight. Villacorta!"

Villacorta ambled up to us.

"Make sure crime scenes doesn't forget the scumbag..."

Villacorta looked at Roberts with a furrowed brow.

"Condom," said Roberts. "Make sure they don't forget the condom in the bathroom trashcan."

Villacorta nodded.

"I want prints on anything and everything."

"You got it," said Villacorta.

"Have housekeeping and the neighbor been interviewed yet?" I asked.

"Gray has them in the next room interviewing them."

I nodded.

"I'd like to go hear what they've got to say."

Roberts nodded.

"Anything else you want to tell me?" I asked him.

He shook his head.

"Can't figure this one out. Looks more like a hit to me. Certainly not a robbery right? I mean why leave a thousand bucks behind?"

"I can think of a thousand reasons to leave it behind," I said to him, grinning.

"Go on then."

"Could be as simple as the killer getting startled during the robbery and getting scared."

"Or it could be a hit," said Roberts.

"Could be that," I replied.

All In: Chapter Two

Room 301 was the spitting image of 303. There were even about the same number of people in them. Roberts and I walked into the room and found a young fat Hispanic woman in her gray and white housekeeping uniform sitting on the bed. Her mascara had run down her cheeks. I think kids nowadays call it the Goth look, but that wasn't her excuse. It was easy to see she had been crying.

Detective Gray was asking her questions as she sat on the bed and he stood in front of her in his blue slacks and blue and red striped shirt. He had brown hair and an angular jaw with piercing green eyes. He was tall and good looking, and I immediately didn't like him. He was the kind of guy who got where he did on looks. That's what I figured. I was wrong.

"Captain," he said, then looking at me. "You Carrick?"

He was smiling a hedgerow of perfect white teeth. I couldn't help but wonder how many baby kittens he had to drown for a set of choppers like that. He reached out a hand which I shook. It was as firm and warm as overcooked steak and just as smooth. I nodded at him.

"I'm a huge fan," he said. "I've studied all your cases."

"Is that so?"

"Yeah. Man, the way you got Goliath to confess on that Gath homicide was off the charts. I'm Lee Gray by the way."

He turned to Captain Roberts.

"Is he helping us out on this one?"

93

Roberts nodded. Gray grinned even wider. I looked harder, and it almost seemed like he had two sets of teeth, a spare just in case.

"Awesome," he said.

I didn't think boys over thirteen said that anymore. I was wrong. I looked at Roberts.

"He reminds me of you. Five and oh is his record."

"Good work," I said, patting him on the back. He grinned at me, and if he was a puppy he probably would have pissed on my leg. What can I say, sometimes I'm wrong about people. I went from zero to liking him in about three seconds.

"What have we got so far?" Roberts asked him.

Gray nodded and looked over at the housekeeper. She was looking down. Her hands in her lap clutched a wet tissue. It wasn't like any origami I had seen.

"Cleofás Jasso, says she was sent up by the manager to check on the noise complaint. When she got here she banged on the door three separate times but the guy never answered. She said the noise was extremely loud so she went downstairs to get Celestino Hernádez, the manager over there."

Gray cocked his head to the short young Hispanic man standing next to him in a black suit that was worse than Villacorta's if that was possible.

"She says he came back up with her and Celestino tried banging on the door three separate times but the guy wouldn't open. Celestino used his manager's key fob to override the door and when they got in they saw the guy lying dead on the floor."

"Did they touch anything?" I asked him.

Gray turned to her and spoke in Spanish. He was asking her what I had just asked him. I don't speak Spanish, but I'm street smart that way. She said something back to him. I looked at him like I'd just been put in the middle of a Pentecostal religious practice of glossolalia.

"She says they didn't touch anything. They went downstairs and called the police and waited for them. They only came back up to open the door for the police."

"When did he arrive?" asked Roberts.

"She doesn't know. Must have been today though, because yesterday the room didn't need cleaning because there was no one in it."

"Carry on," said Roberts, "see what else you can get out of her. We'll talk to the manager."

Gray nodded and turned to the housekeeper. Roberts and I walked up to the short Hispanic guy in a big suit.

"You the manager?" asked Roberts.

He nodded and smiled. He looked us both in the eyes. He was a friendly guy, and you could tell he was eager to help.

"Do you mind stepping over here with me," said Roberts as he led us to the far side of the room for some privacy.

"I'm Captain Roberts, and this is Anthony Carrick," he said.

Hernádez shook our hands warmly as if he were presenting some sort of real estate seminar.

"I'm Celestino," he said. "Celestino Hernádez. Most people think its Hernandez, but my folks dropped the second N when we crossed the border. It was too heavy."

He grinned at us. I smiled back at him. He was a funny guy, and sociable. You could see how he made it to management being so young.

"You've got the same name as that Panamanian boxer Caballero."

"Yeah," he said, nodding. "'Cept I don't box and I'm shorter than him."

I was trying to break the ice, but I figured he'd done a better job of that than me already.

"Your housekeeper said you sent her up here to check on the noise complaint."

Celestino nodded vigorously.

"Yeah, Mr. McSpadden - this is his room - called in a complaint so I had Cleo check it out. She came back and told me the guy wasn't answering so I went upstairs with her and tried myself. I banged three times, really loud, but I got no answer. I announced myself and then used my manager key to open up his door. The TV was on and blaring. That wasn't the first thing I saw though. The first thing was Mr. Hartley dead on the ground with a bullet hole in his forehead."

"Did you touch anything?"

"No way, man. I watch CSI so I know not to disturb the scene. I told Cleo we needed to go call the police so we left the room and went downstairs where we called you guys."

"And the doors to the rooms, they all close by themselves?"

"Yes, I heard it close when we were down the hall a bit."

"Do you know when Hartley signed in?"

"I'd have to check the computer downstairs, but it was today. Around lunchtime."

"How did he pay?"

"With cash. I thought he was crazy, man, he pulled out this huge roll of cash and peeled off two Benjamins. The room's actually $206.75 with taxes but I let is slide. He said he only had Benjamins on him."

I looked at Roberts, and he looked at me.

"He had a variety of bills," Roberts told me. "Mostly twenties, and hundreds, but some fives and tens."

"Oh," said Celestino.

"Had he been here before? Have you seen him anywhere?"

Celestino shook his head.

"No, but I like to talk to my guests when they sign in, if I'm at the front desk, and I was. I saw all that money, like I said, and I asked him what he was doing here. He said he was going to play poker at the Rustler Casino."

"Do you know where he's from?" asked Roberts.

Celestino shrugged his head.

"No. He said he came in by taxi and didn't have a driver's license, so I made up an address for him."

Celestino grinned sheepishly.

"You know you're not supposed to do that."

Roberts frowned at him, but he wasn't the hospitality police, and he didn't really care to be.

"I know, sorry, it won't happen again."

"Did he tell you anything else that might be important."

"Not really, but he appeared to be excited about something. He said he felt lucky, but he kept looking over his shoulder as if he was expecting somebody."

"How busy are you tonight?" asked Roberts.

"Not too busy. We're at about sixty percent occupancy."

"Anybody in 305 or 203?"

"No, they're both still vacant if you're looking for a room."

Celestino grinned and Roberts offered him the smallest of smirks.

"What about across the hall?"

"300 is occupied, but 302 and 304 are empty."

Roberts nodded.

"If you think of anything else," said Roberts, "let Detective Gray know."

Roberts nodded at the young good looking homicide detective who was still trying to wring any last drop of information from the housekeeper.

"Gray will let you know when you can go."

At the far corner of the room on the sofa sat a middle aged guy in a wife beater and gray slacks. His feet were naked. I wished they weren't. The toenails were jaundiced and looked like clamshells. Thick tufts of black wire grew from each toe and a scrambled mess of it carpeted the top of his feet. His forearms, and knuckles were thick with black hair. I figured he was the missing link between Homo erectus and sapiens.

He was a thin, wiry guy with a tight small belly that didn't seem to belong to the rest of him. His hair was a messy black bird's nest and his face was a minefield of spent shells and long ago exploded pockmarks. He looked up at us as we approached him, and that's when I knew how he managed a tight belly on his thin frame. His nose looked like it was stolen from a proboscis monkey. Standing close to him you could smell the sweet, sickly cologne of the alcoholic. He was well on his way to destroying his liver.

"I'm Captain Roberts of homicide."

"Stephen McSpadden," he said, looking up at Roberts.

I walked over to the window and opened the curtains. I peered outside over the parking lot. It was mostly empty but I saw Hartley's blue M5 parked in a corner by itself. I turned around and joined Roberts.

"You called in the noise complaint," said Roberts.

McSpadden nodded.

"Where you in your room all night?"

"No, I got back to the hotel at around twelve thirty. I came up to my room, and tried to go to bed, but the guy was blaring his TV."

"Was it a show?"

"No, I don't think so. It sounded like music. Mostly that shit hip hop and rap."

I smiled at him. That was probably the worst choice for coming to grips with a bender.

"Anyway, I decided I'd have a shower and see if the guy came to his senses. He didn't, so I went over and banged on his door. Friggin' idiot wouldn't open up so that's when I called housekeeping."

"What time was that?"

McSpadden shrugged.

"I don't know. Around one maybe. A little before."

I pulled out my phone and showed McSpadden a picture of Hartley.

"Did you know him?"

"Jesus," he said. "That's the guy?"

He looked up at me, and I figured I'd sobered him up just like that. I nodded.

"Yeah I've seen him?"

"Where?"

"At the Rustler Casino tonight."

"You were there?"

"Yeah, I was playing blackjack. He was making a killing at the poker table. At least that's what he kept telling everyone. You know how you get sore losers?"

I nodded.

"Well, he was a sore winner. Dragging the other players' noses in it. One guy almost went ballistic on him, but security tossed him out. A little while later, he gets tossed out too. Bitching and moaning all the time saying it's because he's winning. But I was grateful they tossed him out, and I reckon a lot of other people were too."

"What time was he tossed out?" asked Roberts.

More shrugging.

"I don't know. It was early. Probably around eleven."

"Was he by himself?"

McSpadden shook his head.

"No, he had some bimbo with him. She must have been a hooker."

"How do you know?" I asked.

McSpadden looked at me as if I'd asked him how he knew the pope was Catholic.

"You could tell. She was probably young enough to be his daughter. She was hardly wearing anything and she had enough makeup on to ice a cake."

"And she left with him?"

"Yeah, she thought the whole thing was quite funny, but they were both drunk. She was leaning on him for support."

"And you're sober?" I asked.

He glared at me from eyes ribboned with red. They were hard eyes, but eyes that had lost their fire.

"I had a few, but nowhere near like them."

Probably more, I figured. But he had years of practice. He was a professional at it. Don't try this at home, kids.

"What brings you to a fine establishment like this?" asked Roberts.

"I'm a salesman. There's a convention in town that I'm here for next week, and I wanted to get some R 'n R in before then."

"What convention is that?"

"RC. I sell remote control toys to small and independent businesses."

"Where you from?" asked Roberts.

"Chicago."

"Did you notice anyone suspicious around the hotel or in the hallway when you got back from the casino?"

McSpadden shook his head.

"No, I just remember hearing that noise coming from his room as I came down the hall. I don't know how long it had been going on for."

Roberts nodded.

"Alright," he said. "Detective Gray will come and get your particulars when he's finished up. He'll let you know when you can go."

McSpadden nodded and Roberts and I walked out of the room. The coroner was hauling Hartley out on a gurney.

"Doctor Proctor," said Roberts, as the coroner walked by, after his assistants.

"Emily's not working tonight, I take it," I said.

"No, she isn't."

He didn't stop to make small talk. He's like that. A guy who's most comfortable in social situations where everyone else is dead.

"He should have been a proctologist," I said to Roberts as we watched him walk down the hall. "It would've suited his name better."

Roberts laughed out loud. I was surprised, I didn't think it was that funny.

"I heard that Tony!" he said.

He knew I didn't like being called Tony. Tony's for Italians and I ain't Italian. But I got the first jab in, so I gave him some slack. Besides, Emily wouldn't appreciate it if I punched her colleague in the mouth. I'd never hear the end of it. Roberts stopped laughing and looked at me.

"What?" I said.

"You like her, don't you?"

"I just think she's a better coroner."

I grinned at him.

"Bullshit," he said. "She's better looking for sure, and you like her."

I shrugged my shoulders.

"We're on a homicide, in case you forgot," I said. "Not a dating convention."

All In: Chapter Three

I followed Roberts to the casino which is up on West Redondo Beach Boulevard. A boulevard whose name I never understood. There's nothing beachy about it. West or East Redondo Beach Boulevard never makes it anywhere near to the beach. The best you get is a shopping mall where you might be able to buy a pair of board shorts. This is how tourists get suckered into paying too much money for crappy hotels.

Rustler Casino is small. They advertise less than one hundred gaming tables. It's for Angelinos who are too lazy to drive the four hours to Las Vegas. How do I know this? Because at two in the morning when we arrived the parking lot was full and people were spilling out onto it like regurgitated maggots.

You might think I'm being too hard on casinos, and you'd be wrong. I had to remortgage my house because I liked gambling too much. I don't have that problem anymore. I'll play poker sometimes but that's not quite the same as gambling. You're playing against other apes instead of the house.

I walked into the brightly lit building and the flashing colors of lights and the sound of bells and whistles. Maybe one in ten of the slots were open. Pensioners with their ashen faces and etched leathery skin sat at them like they were hooked up to lung machines.

We walked up to the cashier and Roberts flashed his badge. He asked to see the manager on duty. We only had to wait a few minutes, but I figured in those few minutes one woman I was watching lost a Jackson.

Roberts and I were ogling an attractive brunette walking up to us. Her legs probably made it to my armpits and her skin was as smooth and brown as honey. Her hair fell around her face and shoulders like a silk waterfall. Her eyes were big and bright and from the V in her blouse two round suns were breaking dawn. I swallowed and steadied my eyes on her face. She was smiling at us as she closed in when we figured out she was the manager.

We steadied ourselves and stood upright. We were now business. She was my height as she took my hand and shook it. Warm and soft as saganaki. I dived into her brown eyes and swam a few laps before she got around to introducing herself to Roberts.

"Rebeca Rodrigues," she said to him. "One C because I'm Brazilian."

"So you're the girl from Ipanema," I said, not being able to help myself.

She looked back at me and smiled politely, indulging my immaturity. She was more business than bikini I was beginning to realize.

"Don't let my good looks fool you, Mr. Carrick, I have an MBA from Harvard," she said to me, smiling.

And you have bosoms from silicon, I thought as I smiled back at her, which might have cost as much as her MBA. Yes, they were that good. She held my gaze for a moment but as her mouth smiled at me her eyes bored into my soul. She'd clean out my wallet at the poker table. I was pretty sure of that. She turned back to Roberts.

"What can I help you with tonight, Captain?"

It was morning, but I wasn't about to correct her. That just would've been petty. Instead I glanced at her round bum as firm as a cherry underneath her gray dress.

"We understand you had an incident here earlier this evening," Roberts said.

"Not something to worry the police about."

"Homicides worry the police, Ms. Rodrigues."

"I see, but we haven't had any homicides here for over a year."

"How comforting," I said, grinning at her.

She glanced at me with her poker face and turned back to Roberts.

"I didn't say you did, Ms. Rodrigues, I was asking about any incidents you might have had earlier."

I pulled out my phone and showed it to her.

"This might jog your memory," I said.

Her poker face cracked ever so slightly, but she recovered quickly.

"This man was here earlier," she said to Roberts, ignoring me.

"Tell me about it."

"Mr. Hartley, I'm assuming you know his name," Roberts nodded, "is a regular. He's a braggart as a winner and even worse as a loser."

"What was he tonight?"

"A terrible winner."

"What happened?"

"He upset a large Russian man who was at the same poker table he was at. He cleaned him out. The Russian was about to teach him a lesson when my security escorted him out."

"Did you happen to get the Russian's name?"

"I think security might have."

Rodrigues turned to the woman behind the cashier.

"Get me Dardan, please," she said.

"And that was the end of it then?"

"No, Mr. Hartley kept getting ruder and drunker as the night wore on. He lost a few games and became belligerent. Then he won a few and became even worse. At that point security asked him to leave."

"And he left quietly?" asked Roberts.

"He did."

"By himself?"

Rodrigues shook her head.

"No, he left with Ruby."

"You know her."

"She works for Rustler Casino. Ruby Aponte's one of the girls who take care of our regulars. But it's not what you think. We run a legal establishment here. She's more of a good luck charm and a companion."

"Is she here?"

Rodrigues nodded.

"I'll get her for you. She arrived back at just after midnight."

"Anything else unusual happen here tonight?"

"Nothing unusual, Captain. We haven't seen the Russian since we escorted him out and obviously Mr. Hartley is dead as Mr. Carrick so kindly pointed out."

She looked at me with a pained expression as if I'd pinched her bum. I hadn't, at least not other than in my mind.

"Anything else?" she asked Roberts.

"No, you've been helpful. I'll be in touch if I need anything else."

She nodded, turned around and walked away. We watched her for a while enjoying the view, until it was blocked by a big redwood of a man.

He put out a huge hairless bear's paw of a hand and I shook it, trying my best to stay planted on the ground. He must have been over six five and he had a blonde crew cut. His face was a square block that had been roughly hewn from some sort of slab of wood.

"Dardan Lakerveld," he said, and he smiled, but his mouth was lost in the great expanse of face. He rolled the vowels around lazily in his mouth before he spat them out. From this I knew he was Dutch.

He took Roberts' hand and gave it a good shake too. I looked him over. He was almost as wide as he was tall, and he was thick with muscle like a prized bull under his blue and white tracksuit. He had a generic face but one that gave no hint to his abilities. No cauliflower ears, no speed bumps on his nose. He had either never been in a fight in his life or he was exceptionally good at fighting. I couldn't tell which, and I didn't want to find out.

"I'm chief security officer for Rustler Casino," he said in his Dutch accent.

I offered him my phone which had the picture of a deceased Hartley on it.

"Was this one of the guys you asked to leave earlier this evening?" I asked.

The blonde giant nodded his head.

"Ja, that's Mr. Hartley. He's a regular and Ms. Rodrigues likes us to treat him softly, but he's an asshole. At least once a month we have to ask him to leave. He upsets the other patrons too much."

"And tonight, what did he do?"

"The same as he always does. If he wins he rubs their noses in it. If he loses he starts swearing at everyone. Tonight he was winning and losing. A Russian went all in and lost to Mr. Hartley. Instead of being gracious he started taunting him. The Russian was about to tear his face off when we had to escort him out. He didn't go gently."

"You had to get rough with him?"

"We had to encourage him, ja."

Dardan grinned at us a knowing grin.

"Ms. Rodrigues said you got his name."

"Ja, that's our policy. If anyone has to be escorted out we have to get their particulars. You know, just in case they want to come back and cause more problems."

"That's smart thinking," said Roberts. "So what's his name?"

Dardan reached into his trouser pocket and pulled out a notepad and looked at it for a moment.

"Alihan Aslakhanov," he said. He spelled it out as Roberts wrote it down.

"You don't happen to have a picture of him do you?"

Dardan smiled and nodded. He fished out a phone from his tracksuit jacket's pocket. He showed us a picture of Alihan. Alihan looked like a thug. His nose was more horizontal than vertical and he had a large scar that went from above his left eyebrow to just above his lip. The left eye was milky blue and obviously blind.

"He looks the part," I said to Roberts.

"Ja," said Dardan. "He knows how to fight, but it's hard to win against the security here at Rustler Casino."

"How many of you helped him out."

"Three of us. We have video if you'd like to see."

That was a generous offer. You don't often get that kind of help from casino security. Most often because they're bigger thugs than their patrons. Roberts nodded.

"I'd like to see that," he said.

"It's in the back," said Dardan.

He turned around and we followed him to the back of the casino and up a flight of stairs. We entered a large comfortable room where a guy in the same style of tracksuit was sitting behind an embankment of monitors. In front of him were one way mirrors that looked over the casino below.

"Bill," said Dardan to the guy in the chair.

Bill looked up at the giant man and nodded.

"Pull up that video of the Russian incident from earlier this evening. These cops want to see it."

Bill looked at us through dead eyes with a poker face before turning back to his terminal. I sized Bill up. He was about my height, five ten, maybe eleven, with a medium build. His left ear was showing the beginnings of a cruciferous vegetable but his nose was straight enough.

"Here it is," he said.

We watched the video. It was in high def and full color. Dardan and Bill came up to the table just as the Russian was about to launch across the table at Hartley. Ruby jumped back slightly, scared, as Dardan and Bill picked Alihan up by the armpits. He settled down and they put him onto his own two feet. As they neared the exit he brought his elbow up real quickly towards Bill's nose, but he blocked it. They got into a scuffle. The Russian moved quickly. He was light on his feet and quick with his hands. A third security member came up and put him into a sleeper hold until he went unconscious. They carried him the rest of the way out. Just outside the entrance, Dardan took out his phone and pointed it at the Russian. The Russian yelled something at them before turning and walking off.

"What was he saying there?" I asked.

Bill turned to me.

"The same as everyone else we have to kick out. He told us he was going to come back with his mates and kick our asses."

I nodded, and turned towards Dardan who was looking over the monitors at the casino floor below us.

"What happened with Hartley later that evening? We heard you had to ask him to leave too."

Dardan nodded slowly but didn't look at me straight away. He had his arms folded across his chest.

"Ja, Mr. Hartley is a handful sometimes, but he spends a lot of money here so we treat him well. But when he starts upsetting too many guests we have to ask him to leave."

Dardan looked at Bill and nodded at him. Bill cued up more video for us.

"Mr. Hartley likes to drink. You know how it is, as long as you're at the table playing you get free drinks. He makes good use of that. We watched him lose a few hands and then win a few hands. He's a nice guy when he's sober, but when he's been drinking he's what you call a mean drunk. Look."

We turned to look at the video Bill had cued up. Hartley was standing and pointing and gesturing at the other players. His face was a mask of ridicule. A third security member we hadn't met yet came up to him. He was a hulking black man with short dreadlocks.

"That's Brandon Jensen," said Dardan behind my left shoulder.

Brandon put a big hand on Hartley's shoulder and whispered something in his ear. Hartley turned around and nodded at him, then he turned back said something else to the other players. Ruby was looking at one of them before she lowered her head and looked away and followed Hartley who had collected his chips.

Brandon escorted Hartley to the cashier where he cashed in all his chips except for one. He peeled some money off the roll and gave it to Ruby. Then Brandon escorted both of them outside. We lost sight of the three of them. A couple of minutes later Brandon came back into the casino where Bill froze the frame.

"He was gone a while," I said.

"Ja, when we escort our guests out who have won a bit of money, we make sure they get out of here safely. Brandon was doing that. We don't want them followed and then carjacked at the first set of lights."

"Ruby works for the casino, right?" I asked.

Dardan nodded.

"So why did she leave with Hartley?"

"It was the end of her shift. She's free to do whatever she wants."

"What about the other players at that table? Any of them regulars?"

Dardan leaned down.

"Go back," he said to Bill.

Bill wound the tape back to Hartley standing and berating the other players. Dardan started pointing at the other players with his finger.

"The Russian isn't a regular. This guy is Mr. Marshall Allen. Not as regular as Mr. Hartley. He comes in about once a month or so to play for a few hours. This guy here is in weekly. His name is Mr. Noah Rowley, he's got an English accent. This guy has come in a few times. Mr. Germain Velázquez. Quiet guy, don't know much about him. Good poker player."

"Does Ruby know him?" I asked.

"I don't think so," said Dardan. "Why?"

"Looks like she's looking at him," I said.

I pointed at her and then at Germain.

"Can you go forward slowly?" I said.

Bill moved the tape forward.

"There," I said. "Looks like she's nodding at him."

Roberts looked at me.

"You think so?"

I nodded.

"Could be the way she's just turning away," he said.

"Could be."

Dardan and Bill didn't say anything.

"Can we speak to her?" I asked, turning to Dardan. He nodded and left to get her.

All In: Chapter Four

"If she just got off shift when she left with Hartley, why is she back here?"

"They'll often come back here if they've forgotten their things," offered Bill.

I looked at him.

"She left with just her handbag," he said, pointing to the video of her leaving with Hartley. "Employees have lockers here and they'll often keep a change of clothes. She probably came back to change."

"And it takes her that long?"

Bill smiled at me indulgently, like I was an infant who needed coddling.

"She's probably waiting for Ms. Rodrigues to get off shift. They're friends and they often carpool together."

"Thanks," said Roberts. "There you go, Anthony. Your conspiracy is a dud."

Dardan walked back into the video room where we were all waiting. Roberts and I were watching the activity below us on the gaming floor. Little ants collecting and tossing away small brightly colored chips. I was bored to tears. I turned to see Dardan walk back in and wondered where Ruby was. She appeared from behind him like a rabbit from a hat.

She was an unnatural blonde, and I didn't hold it against her. Her skin was tanned and warm and it sparkled. Must have been the lotion she had on. She wore black yoga pants and a pink top to match her sandals. She was dolled up and painted like a Barbie doll.

"Ruby?" asked Roberts.

She nodded and bit her lower lip. It might have been cute on a five year old getting into trouble for tearing the head off her doll, but on a thirty-something woman it made me cringe for her. It had the opposite affect on Roberts. He walked up to her like a protective father and offered her his limp hand.

"I'm Captain Roberts from homicide."

"Oh dear," she said, blinking her false eyelashes at him.

She ignored me completely, moving closer to Roberts than was necessary. I could smell her cheap perfume from across the room. She'd probably bathed in it.

"That's Anthony Carrick," he said, nodding in my direction. She didn't look away from him.

"Has something bad happened, Captain?" she asked Roberts, gently touching his forearm. I was rolling my eyes so much I started feeling sick. I moved up to be closer to both of them. I started to pull out my phone and show her the picture of her dead John. Roberts put his arm out, and said it wasn't necessary.

"Can you tell me about your evening with Mr. Hartley?"

Ruby put her hand to her mouth.

"Did something happen to him?" she asked, wide-eyed as a doe staring down the barrel of a hunter.

"I'm afraid so, Ms. Aponte..."

"Please call me Ruby," she said, batting her eyes at him as if they were delicate butterflies.

"Mr. Hartley was murdered tonight," said Roberts as solemnly as he could muster.

"Dear God," said Ruby, "poor Mars."

She batted her eyes and turned on the waterworks. I had a feeling it was all for show, but maybe she did genuinely feel bad for the guy. Roberts put his hand on her shoulder.

"I'm sorry," he said like a caring uncle, "but I need to ask you some questions."

She nodded and squeezed out a few more tears for good measure. If this was a movie I'd have walked out already.

"Tell me what happened tonight?"

Dardan had left again to do something he hadn't bothered telling us about. I didn't care. I wanted to run down the Russian and check out Mr. Velázquez.

"Dardan must have told you about the Russian man who threatened Mars tonight. I thought he was going to kill him."

"What did this Russian say?" asked Roberts.

"He said he was going to get his money back and if he didn't then he said that Mars was a dead man. Do you think he really did it?"

"We're still looking into it. I understand you left with Mr. Hartley at around eleven this evening?"

Ruby nodded and pulled a tissue from under her waistband to dab at her eyes.

"Mr. Hartley was such a nice man. I loved him," she said. "He always treated me so well. I'd been seeing him for a few months, and he wanted to celebrate his winnings this evening with me."

Roberts nodded reassuringly.

"I've been told he was a poor loser but a worse winner."

Ruby smiled.

"He was just misunderstood," she said. "He never meant it. Sometimes he just got a bit excitable when he'd had too much to drink.

"So you went back to his hotel room?"

Ruby nodded and bit her lip again for good measure. Roberts was hypnotized.

"I was just there for a little while. I left sometime after midnight. I was back here by twelve thirty. I'm sure anyone here can verify that."

"Did you notice anything unusual or anyone following you to the hotel room?"

Ruby shook his head.

"I don't think so. Brandon followed us out to make sure. We do that so that our customers aren't robbed out in the parking lot. Mars didn't seem particularly concerned about anyone. I asked him about the Russian, but he just blew it off saying that the guy was just talking big but he wouldn't follow through."

"Thank you, Ruby," said Roberts. "I think that's all."

She nodded and was about to turn around when I stopped her.

"Can you tell me about Germain Velázquez," I said.

She looked me up and down like I was a menu and she wanted a piece of me. I had plenty on offer.

"Who?" she asked, but her hesitation gave her away.

"The man you were making eye contact with before you and Hartley were escorted out."

Roberts looked at me as if I'd just gone mad.

"I'm sorry, I don't know who you mean."

She was trying to play me like a cheap fiddle. But there were two problems with that. I wasn't cheap and I wasn't a fiddle. I turned to Bill.

"Can you bring up that video again?" I asked him. He did as I asked. I pointed at the man with slicked back black hair and a well groomed goatee.

"That Mr. Velázquez," I said.

"Oh, yes, I know him. He's fairly regular but I'm not looking at him."

"I see," I said, looking right through her at her black heart.

"You'll have to excuse my partner, he gets grumpy when he hasn't had his beauty sleep."

She smiled at Roberts and batted her eyes before turning around and walking her tight ass out of the room. I liked her better from the back. She wasn't lying to me then. We made our way out after verifying that she did in fact reenter Rustler Casino at twelve thirty-seven a.m. Whether that was an alibi was yet to be determined.

"I sometimes wonder why I bring you along with me," said Roberts in all seriousness.

"Because I make you look good," I said.

"I'm serious," he said.

I stopped and looked at him and thought for a moment.

"I never left a case unsolved," I said. "Sometimes you've gotta think with your big head, Johnny. You're still too sentimental and soft when it comes to a damsel in false distress."

I walked away letting him think about that. I lit up a cigarette and decided a Scotch was my best option for the rest of the evening.

All In: Chapter Five

I try to get up before noon. Seems to me if I can do that, then the day's not wasted. Today was not a good day. Teacher's had put me through a mean class last night. In short I had been schooled again by a Scotch whisky. Teacher's Highland Cream Perfection, and about the only perfect thing about it was the headache I was nursing.

I got up out of bed after slithering underneath the tattered fur ball of Pirate. The cat opened his one good eye and looked at me as if I was mad to be getting up so early. I reached for my phone and saw the time was twelve eleven. Almost made it out of bed before noon. It wasn't that bad all things considered. It was a Saturday after all.

I took a shower, a gallon of water and a bottle of aspirin. And by the time I stepped out of the bathroom clean-shaven I was starting to feel like I'd only been run over by a go-kart. Roberts had called and left a message at eight. I listened to it. He said if I was interested he'd be interviewing Hartley's widow, Michelle, at one. I had to put some pep in my step, it was already quarter to. I fed Pirate, and walked out of my apartment wondering what the hell I'd done with my car.

My car was perfectly parked in my stall. In fact it had been reversed in. I scratched my head. There was no way in hell I'd have parked it that way in the state I must have been in. I got in and drove off towards Valley Village, when it started to come back to me. I remembered calling a driving service on the insistence of the barkeep at the Royal Cock. They'd driven me home. Reversing into my stall was a nice touch. I think I'd use them again, if I ever had another drink.

I rolled down the windows because it was hot. The radio announcer said it was eighty-five already and I felt it. A/C would've been nice but it was acting up. I was left with the only other option.

Valley Village was about a half hour away from where I was in Santa Monica. That meant I was gonna be late. Interesting thing about Valley Village is it used to be part of North Hollywood, but in the eighties much of San Fernando Valley wanted to create its own identity not associated with tinsel and tans. In the early nineties Valley Village got its way, and became a distinct community.

Not that you care, but I'm trying to fill in the time it takes for me to reach the Hartleys. Valley Village is what I'd call a lower middle income community. Most folks are renters and most are old for Angelinos, at an average age of thirty-six. That means in these parts I'm Methuselah.

I parked outside the five story apartment block and put out my cigarette. I walked into the lobby and buzzed 101. A woman let me in without even checking who I was. But then I figured she probably had Roberts with her. I was right.

It was ten after when she let me into the apartment. She was an average sized woman, thicker around the middle than she needed to be. She wore too much makeup, too much perfume and not enough clothes. Her blouse was open too low and her chest was freckled with liver spots and as loose as a turkey's wattle. I smiled at her and introduced myself to her as if she were the most charming woman in the world. She took to me like a bee to a flower.

I nodded at Roberts and he gave me a curt not back. I could tell he was still sore. I sat down on the worn couch next to him. In front of me was a coffee table. There was a clean mug, a pot of coffee and assorted cookies on it. Michelle invited me to have some. Coffee was exactly what I needed so I indulged her.

"Did I miss much?" I asked.

"We were just getting down to it. Mrs. Hartley was kind enough to make us some coffee."

I smiled at her, and she puffed up like a peacock. She was much like her late husband. Not that attractive but using all manner of paint, dye and preening to do the best she could with what she had. Her hair was brassy blonde, a thick crown around her head in large curls that looked carved from a cylinder of brass. I didn't know if this was a bereavement call or if she already knew. I figured we were the grim reaper's time keepers.

"Is everything alright with Marsden?" she asked.

She didn't know. I cursed under my breath. This had been the worst part of my job. I loathed having to inform the families of the death of their loved ones.

"I'm afraid that's why we're here, ma'am," said Roberts.

"Please call me Michelle," she said, and I could already see her veneer crack like a cheap LA highway.

"I'm afraid your husband was found murdered early this morning," said Roberts.

I took a sip of my coffee and swallowed hard. We all waited for a while to let it sink in. Michelle nodded. She swallowed a thick wad of hurt down into her gut, and her eyes teared up.

"Could you excuse me for a moment?"

She didn't wait for Roberts' response. She left the dining room and disappeared down the hallway. I looked at Roberts and he looked at me back. I took a cookie and ate it. I listened to the traffic whirring by, oblivious to the unfolding chaos all about us. And I knew that this one, this time I would get justice. Even if Marsden had been a prick.

After a few minutes, Michelle came back into the room wearing a brave smile that kept slipping off. She dabbed at her eyes, redder than mine. Roberts smiled at her.

"We're very sorry for your loss, Michelle," he said.

He was good at this sort of thing. Better than I was. I felt like folding myself up and tucking myself away under the sofa cushions. Roberts waited for a moment. Michelle took a sip of coffee.

"As you must know," Roberts continued, "we need to ask a few questions if you don't mind."

The brave smile and a nod of the head. Roberts was about to enter a minefield. How much of her husband's philandering was she aware of? How was he going to handle this hornet's nest?

"Can you tell me what your husband was doing last night?"

That was a gentle, wide open question. He was good. That's why he was captain.

"Once a month he liked to go gambling. He said he was going to be spending the weekend at the Rustler Casino. He usually finds a cheap hotel somewhere nearby."

"Your husband was a veteran," said Roberts. "I understand he was discharged with a small pension after suffering injuries in Afghanistan?"

Michelle nodded.

"He was so proud of his service. He made major, but he didn't like being at headquarters when his men were out there. He wanted to join them, and so he did, but that's what got him injured. He could have stayed on doing paperwork but that wasn't his thing so he decided to get pensioned out."

"I'd like you to help me understand your financial situation. Your husband drives a 2005 M5, which is not a cheap car, and, if you'll forgive me, you live in Valley Village in a one bedroom apartment. A military pension can't be much more than about three grand. How did your husband afford his car for instance?"

122

"You're right, Captain," she said. "The pension wasn't much. Less than three thousand per month, and I don't work, because Marsden didn't want me to. I offered but he wouldn't hear of it. That's just the way he was, but it bothered me. He's never been consistent with winning. The car for instance he won in 2005, his first year out of the army, at a local poker tournament. And frankly that didn't help him, because it made him feel like he was some sort of poker star. But he lost more often than he won."

"I'm sorry," said Roberts. "That must be difficult."

"It is," said Michelle, dabbing at her eyes again. "He was a good man until his injury in Afghanistan. Something happened to him over there. And I don't just mean the physical injury. I sometimes wonder if a part of his mind or soul was left there. He was never the same when he came back. He was moody and angry and he took to drinking and gambling. He'd never gambled before. Not more than the occasional poker night with the boys."

Roberts nodded as I drank my coffee and ate a second jam filled cookie.

"We noticed that he was wearing a NY Giants' Super Bowl ring."

Michelle nodded and smiled weakly.

"He was proud of that. Prouder than winning the car really. He won that in a celebrity tournament at the final table against Larry Baines. Larry was very upset about it."

"Where you there?"

"No, but Marsden told me about it. He thought that Larry was going to punch him in the face afterwards. But you have to understand that Marsden wasn't the most gracious loser, or winner for that matter."

"That's what we hear. Do you know of anyone who might have wanted him killed?"

"Not really, though like I said, Larry Baines was quite upset but I suppose he could have just bought the ring back from

Marsden, though that's probably unlikely. I don't think Marsden would have parted with it for all the gold at Fort Knox."

"Anyone else you can think of?"

"No, I'm afraid not, Captain. Sadly, Marsden and I had started to drift apart, especially a few months ago. Something happened and he just got more withdrawn and angry. We started getting hang up phone calls. Eventually he told me just to stop answering the phone. He thought they were probably just telemarketers but we never had that sort of thing before. But I didn't press him, it would have just made him madder. Then just this week I received notice from the management company that we're three months behind in rent and if we don't pay up in full by the end of the month we'll be evicted."

Michelle teared up again and fought it back. She dabbed at her eyes and crumpled up the tissue in her lap when she was done. She pinched her lips together to stem the flow. I started squirming inside. The poor woman was about to become destitute and homeless and there wasn't a thing I could do. I was barely making rent myself.

"And you don't know exactly what happened to him a few months ago that changed his behavior for the worse?"

"No, I'm sorry. Marsden and I haven't really been communicating very well for a while. I was fearful that he was getting into trouble with his gambling habit. Do you think that might have happened?"

"I can't say for certain, Michelle. That's certainly one option that we're looking into. Though interestingly nothing was stolen from your husband."

"I've just had a thought," I said, blurting it out.

They both looked at me with surprise as if they'd forgotten I was in the same room as them.

"This isn't quite related to the murder, but I'd hate to see Michelle lose her home."

Roberts nodded at me.

"I was thinking. She'd get her husband's property once the case has been solved right?"

Roberts nodded again.

"That Larry Baines' ring has got to be worth at least fifty grand. If Larry turns out not to be the murderer, would you be willing to sell it back to him?"

I looked at Michelle. She nodded and smiled more confidently.

"That way everyone wins. Larry gets his ring back and Michelle gets to keep her home," I said. "Lawrence Taylor's ring sold at auction for almost a quarter of a mill. If Larry gets his ring back for fifty, he's made a deal."

"And what if he doesn't want to pay that much?" asked Roberts.

"Then you put it up for auction. If Taylor's can go for almost that much, I'm sure Baines' could fetch at least a hundred grand."

Roberts looked at Michelle and she smiled at him.

"I'd be happy to let him have it back for fifty thousand," she said, and for the first time that day I saw her smile genuinely.

"Yes," said Roberts, "that's all well and good. But even if we get a quick conviction on this case, it'll be several months before the property is eligible to be released."

"I've thought of that too. Michelle and Larry sign an agreement. Larry pays her now and she signs over the rights of release for the ring to him. Then LAPD releases the ring to Larry when the time comes."

"I suppose that would work," said Roberts. "In the meantime, can we get back to solving the case?"

I nodded and picked up a third cookie. I was feeling good about the progress of things now that I didn't have to worry about Michelle. Roberts looked at Michelle for a moment before he spoke.

"I'm afraid I have to ask you a delicate question," he said. He paused further.

"Do you think your husband might have been having an affair?"

Michelle didn't flinch. She shrugged her shoulders.

"I wouldn't be surprised. We hadn't been intimate for quite some time. But if he was he was being discreet. Did you find evidence to suggest it?"

"Yes, we have," said Roberts emboldened by Michelle's lack of shyness. "It appears he might have been carrying on with one of the female staff at Rustler Casino."

Michelle nodded and looked past Roberts and out across the street.

"He wasn't the man I had fallen in love with twenty-five years ago," she said absentmindedly.

All In: Chapter Six

I was standing outside the Hartleys' apartment complex talking with Roberts. The sun was blistering sweat along my hairline and my shirt felt slightly sticky against my back.

"I think I'm starting to get a feel for this," I offered Roberts.

"How's that?"

"I think Hartley was in to some loan shark for a chunk of change and that got him killed."

Roberts shook his head.

"That makes no sense to me," he said. "Why kill the guy if he owes you money, and then you don't even take what he has on him."

I shrugged. Sometimes murder didn't need to be neat and tidy. I could think of a bunch of reasons why something like that might go south. None of which I wanted to share with Roberts. His phone rang as we stood there loitering. He hung up after just a few exchanges.

"Baines is coming down the station, and they've picked up the Russian."

"Your guys are worth their salt," I said.

I followed Roberts back to the administration building. We parked outside and walked in. Up in homicide Roberts led me to an interview room. A large and reasonably well-kept Larry Baines was sitting with his lawyer waiting for us. We sat down opposite them.

"Thank you for coming in Mr. Baines," said Roberts.

Baines rubbed his right finger where his Super Bowl ring used to be. He smiled at us.

"Always happy to help the LAPD."

"I'm just going to get down to the facts," said Roberts. "I don't want to waste any more of your time than needed."

"I appreciate that."

"It's about Marsden Hartley," said Roberts.

"What does that idiot want now?" asked Baines.

Baines' lawyer laid his hand on his client's forearm, and gave him a look.

"He was murdered."

"Oh, I see," said Baines. "Was my ring taken?"

"Tell me about that," said Roberts. "How did your ring end up on Hartley's finger."

"He won it at a tournament. I got carried away, and instead of walking away I sold it to him for twenty five grand so I could get back in the game."

"I didn't know you could get buy ins that late in a tournament," I said.

Baines looked at his lawyer and his lawyer nodded at him.

"It wasn't that kind of tournament. More like off the books."

"What were you doing last night at between eleven and one in the morning?" asked Roberts.

"I was home with my wife."

Not the best alibi that I'd heard in my career, but it was better than nothing. And somehow he didn't strike me as a murderer.

"So when I can get my ring back?" he asked.

"Well, that's the problem," I said. "It's no longer your ring, you sold it. The rightful owner is now Mrs. Hartley. But she's in a spot and will sell it back to you."

"I'll give her twenty five for it," he said.

Baines was relaxed in the interview room. If he had killed Hartley he was most certainly a cool psychopath. But I didn't like him for it.

"You're obviously not up on current commodity spot prices. I reckon a ring like yours could probably fetch close to a quarter mill. Just like Taylor's did recently."

Baines was a poker player but his poker face was starting to slip.

"I'm not gonna pay that kind of money to get my ring back. I'll give her fifty."

He didn't take me for a haggler but I was feeling ornery. The edges of my headache were scratching at the outside of my skull.

"I think a hundred would be a steal."

"I didn't think I'd be getting robbed by LAPD homicide detectives."

"I'm not with the LAPD," I said.

"Fine, my last offer is seventy five."

"Sold," I said. "But here's the thing. You pay Mrs. Hartley now and you get the ring back when this whole case is wound its way through court. Your lawyer can write up the agreement for Mrs. Hartley to sign."

Baines looked at his lawyer who shrugged with his palms up.

"Fine," he said.

"I'm going to ask you directly if you killed Marsden Hartely, Mr. Baines," said Roberts.

"No I didn't. I was with my wife when, I'm assuming, he was killed."

"You know how this works," said Roberts, "I have to ask. We've heard from a witness that you got pretty upset when Hartley got to keep your ring."

Baines looked at his lawyer again, and the puppet nodded his head.

"I told him he'd better let me win my ring back, but we've never had the chance. He kept stalling on a rematch. I think he wanted to keep it."

"So now that he's dead, that works out well for you," said Roberts.

"Not really, it's cost me fifty grand to get it back. If I'd have killed him I'd have taken the ring off his finger."

"I think we're done here, gentleman," said the lawyer in his banker's pin striped suit. "Unless you're going to arrest my client, we'll be leaving."

The two of them got up and walked out of the room.

"Thanks for coming in, Mr. Baines," said Roberts. Baines looked back at him and nodded. Then they disappeared through the door.

"I don't think he did it," said Roberts.

"I think you're a genius," I said to him, grinning.

"Captain," said Detective Gray, coming up to us. "Alihan Aslakhanov is ready for an interview."

Roberts nodded and we followed Gray down the hall to another interview room. We walked in and sat down. Aslakhanov was seated across from us. He didn't look happy, but that just might have been his beaten up face and sideways nose. Roberts opened up a folder that Gray had given him and scanned it quickly. He took a photo out of the folder. It was of Hartley before he was dead. Probably taken from the DMV. He pushed it towards Aslakhanov.

"You know this man?" asked Roberts.

Aslakhanov looked at it briefly and shook his head. His arms were crossed in front of himself.

"Don't start off lying, because that's a quick trip to cells and a murder charge."

Aslakhanov looked up at us a little more carefully now.

"You're saying he's dead?" he asked. His accent was Russian but he enunciated well.

"That's exactly what I'm saying. Do you want to come clean?"

"Alright, alright," said Aslakhanov, "I know him, we played poker last night."

Roberts nodded.

"That's better. It says here," said Roberts, looking down at the folder in front of him, "that you boxed for the Russian army."

Aslakhanov laughed out loud. I didn't follow what was so funny.

"You Americans," he said. "You have no idea how the world works."

"Then why don't you enlighten us."

"I boxed in the Chechen army, and fought against the Russians."

"However interesting that might be," said Roberts, "I'm not all that interested. You came here on a Russian passport in ninety-nine, and got citizenship the next year. That's the summary. But what I'm really interested in is why you killed this man here."

Roberts pushed his index finger into Hartley's forehead where the bullet had gone.

"I didn't kill him," said Aslakhanov.

"You're going to have to do better than that," said Roberts. "Let me refresh your memory."

Roberts pulled out a still we had obtained from Rustler Casino before we left. It showed an angry Aslakhanov practically launching himself across the poker table at Hartley. Roberts put this photo on top of the one of Hartley. Aslakhanov looked down at it.

"This is just a misunderstanding," he said, shrugging his knotted shoulders and smiling at us.

"Well," said Roberts, "you better start helping me understand it. I'm getting tired of your half-assed answers."

Roberts looked at him and held his stare.

"Okay, okay," said Aslakhanov. "This guy Marsden, he was an asshole. He kept baiting everyone at the table. If he won he rubbed it in your face. If he lost he told you what a loser you were. I had enough. He'd just taken all my chips, and he was laughing in my face. He said to me. He said 'you Russians are nothing but alcoholic losers who screw your own sisters'. So yes. He took my money and insulted me. You don't do that in Russia. I wanted to teach him a lesson. But security grabbed me before I could punch that smile off his face."

"So you followed him back to the hotel and then waited until the woman he was with left. Then you got into his room and shot him."

Aslakhanov leaned back and put his hands up as if to surrender.

"No, I didn't. I mean, yes, I wanted to teach him a lesson. He won the game fair, but he insulted my sister. I wasn't going to let that stand. So I waited, and then later he came out with that whore he was with. But he had one of those security guys with him too. The security guy waited while they got into the car. Marsden was drunk. I don't know why they let him drive off. He was taking forever to get into his car. I was waiting. You see at first I just wanted to mess him up a bit in the parking lot, but the security guy was on him like a second coat. So I got into my car to wait. Then I see this other guy come out of the casino and get into his car. I don't like the look of him. He looks like trouble. He looks at me as if to say to back off. He's a small guy, but I can tell he'd sooner cut you as talk to you. This guy follows Marsden and the whore he's with and I decide I don't want to get involved in what's going on with that."

"Can you describe this guy to us?" asked Roberts.

"I can show you him," said Aslakhanov. "This is him here."

Aslakhanov puts his dirty, oil stained finger on the photo of the poker table. When he lifts his finger off, we can see who he's been pointing at. I look at Roberts knowingly.

"What was he driving?" I asked.

"A black Chrysler 300 SRT."

"What did you do after you decided Hartley wasn't worth your trouble?" asked Roberts.

"I went to a bar close by and stayed until around two. You can check with the bartender."

"What bar was this?"

"Reggie's Sports Bar."

Roberts nodded, and looked out the door to the officer who was standing out there. The uniform came into the room.

"This officer will show you out. Don't go too far," said Roberts.

Aslakhanov stood up and nodded and was led out of the room by the uniform. I turned to Roberts.

"I told you Ruby wasn't on the up and up."

Roberts didn't say anything to me. He stood up and we walked out. He went over to the desk where Villacorta and Gray were seated.

"I want us to start moving more quickly on this. Check out Aslakhanov's alibi. He says he was at Reggie's Sports Bar until around two. That's up there on West Redondo by Van Ness. I want you to pick up a Germain Velázquez and bring him in. Look into Ruby Aponte. I want backgrounds on both of them. I also want to find out if Baines was at home with his wife like he says he was."

Villacorta and Gray nod. They get up and head out. Roberts turns to me, and he's not smiling.

"So what's your big idea?" he asked.

"I was thinking of opening a tiki bar by the pier if I can get it past the red tape."

"Smart ass," he said.

"I don't have a big idea, John. I just know that batting-eyed Ruby's not been straight with us."

"So you think she killed him?"

I shook my head.

"I didn't say that. I'm just saying there's more we can squeeze out of her. And I want to know about her relationship with Germain."

"I don't get it," said Roberts. "If they'd been in on it, why wasn't anything stolen from Hartley."

"Those are the questions we need to get the answers to."

All In: Chapter Seven

I had left Roberts at headquarters and driven down to the pier where I spent the rest of my day watching the fat tourists get fatter and redder eating ice cream and flopped out on the beach like seals. I was trying to figure out the murder angle. Why kill a guy and not take his Super Bowl Ring or the grand in his wallet? Something was going on that I couldn't quite see.

So I headed to a local pub and had a steak sandwich and a couple of beers. Scotch and I weren't on speaking terms. Though I was pretty sure I'd get over it.

Ten the next morning I found myself back at police headquarters sitting across from Roberts. It felt just like old times.

"I think we've gotta cast our net wider to find this fish," I said to him.

We were waiting for Gray and Villacorta to get back. They were bringing in Germain and Ruby. I was drinking an extra strength Americano. I'd given Roberts a regular coffee.

"What do you mean?"

"I think we should look into Hartley's background. You see, I was out by the pier yesterday after I left, and I was watching these tourists get fat and red in the hot sun. I got to asking myself why are they here? What's so special about Santa Monica? And then it dawned on me. Maybe there's nothing special about Santa Monica. Maybe they ended up here not for surfing or for Hollywood. Hell, maybe they didn't come specifically to LA."

Roberts was shaking his head at me and grinning. He took a sip of his coffee.

"How much did you have to drink last night?"

"Not enough, that's why I'm so clear headed and erudite," I said to him. "Seriously though, maybe these tourists have come here to visit family or friends. Or maybe they just came out here because it was the cheapest place for a holiday. Why they're here has nothing to do with LA or Santa Monica. What I'm saying is, maybe Hartley's murder has got nothing to do with gambling. Maybe we're looking up the wrong ladder."

"Not a bad idea," Roberts said. "Let's see what falls from the tree after we've spoken with Ruby and Germain."

I nodded. We ended up in silence, enjoying our coffee, and me feeling like a sore thumb someplace I hadn't been a part of for years. It wasn't long before Gray and Villacorta came back with Germain and Ruby. They took them into two separate rooms and came back out lonely.

"Seems those two do know each other. We found her at his apartment," said Gray.

"Yeah, we got a two for one deal for that trip," said Villacorta.

"What's in his jacket?" I asked.

Villacorta looked at me funny, like I was a grandfather using teenage slang.

"He's got priors for battery, robbery, assault and a few misdemeanor pimping charges," said Gray. "We also picked up a Glock 30."

"That takes a .45. Same as what killed Hartley," said Roberts. Gray nodded.

"What about Ruby Tuesday?" I asked.

"A couple of prostitution misdemeanors, paid by her pimp, Germain," said Gray.

"What did I say?"

I looked at Roberts and he shrugged.

"Nothing worth listening to. Let's go hear what she has to say. You guys see what you can find out about Germain," Roberts said to Gray and Villacorta.

I walked with Roberts to the interview room which held Ruby. I looked at him and stopped before we walked in.

"You up for this? You think you can be impartial?" I asked, grinning at him.

"Depends what she's offering up," he said to me, winking.

We walked in and Ruby looked up and smiled sweetly at the Captain. She batted her eyelids for good measure too.

"Captain," she said, and she almost sounded excited to see him again.

Roberts wasn't having any of it. He sat down without looking at her and opened up a folder. After a few seconds of silent pause during which I eyeballed her and she kept her eyes on Roberts, he looked up at her.

"I tried to play nice the first time we spoke, Ms. Aponte. I gave you every opportunity to be honest with me. Instead you lied to my face. And now you're in here facing murder charges, and next door is your pimp. How long do you think he's going to sit there before he folds like a used condom and gives you up."

Ruby started to cry. This time I didn't know if it was real or forced. Maybe she was finally getting scared. As she should.

"Now I don't believe you killed him, but I think you had something to do with it. Still that makes you an accessory. And if you help me out, I'll speak to the DA on your behalf."

Ruby shook her head.

"I didn't shoot him, I swear it. Germain didn't shoot him either," she said.

"That's hard to believe, Ms. Aponte, because when we picked you two up we also found a Glock 30. That's the same kind of gun that was used to kill Mr. Hartley."

Ruby started getting hysterical, saying she didn't do it. Saying Germain didn't do it. I told her to get a hold of herself.

"You're going to have to help us out or things are looking real bad for you," I said.

She stopped crying for a moment and I looked at her scary clown face with black mascara streaked down from her eyes. She dabbed at them with a tissue she had up her sleeve.

"I can't tell you what happened because I'll get into trouble," she said. "You don't know what he's like."

"If you don't tell us, we're going to charge you with murder. That's gonna be a lot worse," I said.

She breathed hard a few times, and nodded her head.

"But you have to swear not to tell him," she said.

I nodded my head.

"Okay. Germain wanted to rob him. He had his gun in his car, and the deal was, I was going to go upstairs and have sex with Mars and get him more drunk and then I was going to leave and get Germain and let him back in so we could rob him. I had to do it or Germain was going to beat me. I had no choice."

"So what happened?" asked Roberts.

"Well, I left the room telling Mars that I needed to get something from the store in the lobby. When I came back with Germain we opened the door to Mars' room and saw that he had been shot dead. He was just lying there on the floor. We panicked and ran out. Germain took me back to the casino. We didn't even think of robbing him because we knew it would look bad and we knew the cops were coming."

"What time was this?" asked Roberts.

"Just after midnight. I was only gone maybe five minutes."

"Did you see anything or anyone when you left to get Germain?"

"Well yeah, there was this one guy who was coming down the hallway, and I passed him. He was kinda scary looking. His face was all scarred up..."

"Like he had been cut?" I asked.

Ruby shook her head.

"No, like acne scars."

I turned to Roberts and he nodded at me.

"And when you came back up with Germain, did you see this man again?"

Ruby shook her head.

"No, we didn't see anyone else. But I thought I heard the door next to Mars room close as we came up the hallway, but that might just be my imagination."

"Okay," said Roberts. "You wait here. If Germain tells the same story you'll be free to go."

Roberts and I got up and exited the interview room. Ruby was looking at her lap when we left. We walked into the observation room where, behind the one way mirror, Gray and Villacorta were interrogating Germain.

"You better start helping yourself here, Germain," said Villacorta. "We've got your Glock and we're testing it. It carries the same .45s that were used to shoot Hartley."

"I'm telling you I didn't do it," he said, his cool façade starting to crack a little under the pressure.

"Listen," said Gray, "my captain's in the other room speaking with Ruby. You think she's gonna say the same thing."

"If she ain't lying she'll say the same thing. Like I told you, we were gonna rob him, I'll admit to that. But when we got to the room he was already dead. We got the hell out of there, man. I knew the cops would be coming and we didn't take nothing because how'd that look if you found his ring on me when you came and picked me up?"

"Ballistics will tell us if your gun was used to shoot him," said Villacorta. "And ballistics doesn't lie."

Roberts knocked on the mirrored window.

"Good," said Germain, "then I'm free to go, because I haven't used that gun in a long time."

Villacorta and Gray walked out of the interview room and came round to where we were. Germain was left alone in the small room looking around for something to grab his attention. Problem was, these rooms were kept sparse and drab on purpose, to get him to sweat a little.

"Is he saying he saw a guy with bad skin?"

Villacorta shook his head.

"No, but he's saying he heard the neighbor's door close just as they were walking up the hallway towards the victim's room."

"Did he say which side of the hallway it was?"

Gray nodded.

"Same side as Hartley's. Figure it's probably room 301."

"That's where McSpadden was staying," said Roberts. "I want you to get back to that hotel and scour McSpadden's room again. I want the murder weapon, and I want everything you can get on him and get it to me by the end of the day."

Villacorta and Gray nodded and left the room. I looked at Roberts.

"I think we're getting somewhere now," I said to him.

He nodded thoughtfully.

"But we've gotta figure out motive here. Without that we might not have anything."

"Motive or weapon," I said. "If we find the murder weapon and it's got his prints on it, to hell with motive, that's enough to hang him."

Roberts looked at me for a while.

"I'd still like motive," he said.

"I gave up on motive a long time ago. Sometimes people just do bad things because they can, or they get caught up in the moment. Looking for motive all the time will drive you mad, John. It near ruined me. It's nice to make sense of the screwed up world we live in, but sometimes things are just unraveling into chaos."

"I hear you, but I think there's motive here someplace."

"You're probably right. Maybe they were army buddies and McSpadden has a hate on for Hartley. Your guys will find a connection. I'd much rather like evidence, it's easier that way than trying to coerce a confession. You'll call me when you have something on him?"

Roberts nodded and I left the room and the police building and walked to my car. I drove down to the pier to watch people again. It was another hot day. Young woman in torn jean shorts and tank top rollerbladed by me and I felt better for a bit. Youth is optimistic, supple and oblivious to the decay that's ever trying to creep further in from the sidelines.

I smiled at a young woman in a summer dress walk by with her dog. She was young and blonde and her skin as soft as pudding. She smiled back at me and I let her walk on by. I'd had enough of plucking flowers only to watch them die in my hands.

All In: Chapter Eight

Sunday evening was as quiet as church. I decided to finish my painting and make an early night of it. That worked out perfectly because at eight on Monday morning I got a call from Roberts. It woke me up.

"Is it even morning?" I asked him.

"Have you even gone to bed yet?" he asked.

I leaned up on my elbow and opened my eyes.

"You've obviously got good news," I said.

"We're going to wrap up this case, Anthony. You wanna come in and be a part of that and earn another couple of hundred dollars?"

"You always know how to push my buttons," I said.

Thanks to the good citizens of Los Angeles I had already earned five hundred bucks off of them. Today would be another two fifty and rent could be paid. I would live to die another day.

"Alright," said Roberts, "I'll see you in ten."

"More like at ten," I said.

"Early bird gets the worm, if he's brought in I'm gonna wrap it up tight without you."

"Fine, I'll see you in an hour."

He hung up and I got out of bed and sat on the edge of it for a moment. I thought about having a cigarette but decided against it. Time was of the essence. I went into the kitchen to feed Pirate so he'd give me some peace in the bathroom. He could wail and meow and cry like the best of them if he thought service was slow. In fairness, from his perspective it probably was.

I was in my car by eight thirty, which meant I was going to get there before nine. Wonders never cease. But then I got stuck in traffic and ended up at police headquarters a little after nine.

I found Roberts in his office going over some paperwork. He looked up from his desk and grinned at me.

"You're late," he said.

"Got stuck in traffic."

"Yeah, I thought you might have forgotten about that one now you're self-employed."

"Self-employed bum you mean."

"Hey, I keep you in the lifestyle you've become accustomed to."

"I'd rather become accustomed to something a little more upscale."

I sat down across from him.

"What have you got?" I asked.

"Motive," he said.

"Just like you wanted."

"Yeah, McSpadden's boy, Stephen junior was under Hartley's command and it appears McSpadden held Hartley accountable for his son's death."

"What happened?"

"The son was in Afghanistan and Hartley sent them in for a sweep when they were ambushed. The six of them were killed by Afghani rebels. McSpadden wrote at least half a dozen letters, from what I can see, to the Army asking for Hartley's termination and restitution for his son."

"I thought the Feds paid death benefits for those killed in action."

"They do, but in this case the money goes to McSpadden's grandson who it appears he never gets to see. It's a bit of dog's breakfast. Stephen junior has a son called Aiden out of wedlock.

From all accounts Aiden's mother moved on to Colorado and he lost contact with her and his son."

"There's probably a story there," I said.

"There is. We were called on a couple occasions for domestics, but no charges were ever laid. Seems she might have left him for that."

I nodded. If only the world were a little more reasonable. If it were, I'd be homeless.

"So the kid, Aiden, is getting the benefits."

"Yeah, with his mother apparently holding it in trust. I imagine old man McSpadden's not gonna like that."

"Did he make any threats?" I asked.

"Sort of."

"What do you mean sort of?"

"Well his final letter to the Army and Veteran's Affairs says that if Hartley isn't going to have to pay with his career then he should pay with his life. But the guy I spoke to said they get this kind of thing all the time from grieving relatives. Especially fathers. They can't take them all seriously."

"And I suppose the icing on the cake is that McSpadden owns a .45?"

"An M1911A1. Irony is, it's not his own. At least not directly. It was his son's and he managed to get ownership of it when his son was KIA."

"I love irony," I said. "So old man McSpadden thinks justice is served by killing his son's commander with his son's own gun. I bet that gave him great pleasure."

Roberts nodded.

"Probably. Villacorta and Gray are out picking him up now. Thing is, old man McSpadden's whole life went sideways after his son's death in 2001. His wife left him, he lost his job and as you could probably tell he's been hitting the sauce pretty hard. You must have smelt it on him when we interviewed him."

I nodded.

"I did. But something else concerns me. He said he only got back to the hotel at around twelve thirty."

"I thought you might say that," said Roberts, handing me a picture to look at.

It showed what looked to be McSpadden leaving the casino just after Hartley. Roberts handed me another one. This one showed McSpadden entering the hotel at eleven seventeen.

"Looks like him," I said, "but I wouldn't want the DA to rest his case on it."

Roberts nodded at me.

"Yeah, but we'll show that to him and he'll fold like fresh laundry. And if we get the M1911 we're golden. Besides, I've got a good feeling that McSpadden isn't going to need much goading to get this off his chest. A guy like that. I reckon he's proud of what he's done."

"You might be right," I said. "When are your guys coming back?"

"When they find him. You got a hot date or something."

I grinned at him.

"Something," I said.

All In: Chapter Nine

Villacorta and Gray were having a harder time finding old man McSpadden and so Roberts and I went to lunch. We went outside and walked around a bit until we found a hot dog stand that offered us a decent bratwurst in a bun.

We sat outside for a while in the shade enjoying our brats and trying not to spill mustard on our shirts. It was working out pretty good. Cops of all flavors came in and out of police headquarters as if the building was breathing them in and out. Uniforms, plainclothes and SWAT, along with some brass. We paid them no attention.

"How is it going in homicide?" I asked Roberts.

"Good enough," he said, taking a bit of his brat. "This Lee Gray chap, like I said, reminds me a lot of you in the early days. I think he's gonna have a good clearance record."

"Times have changed," I said. "Back in the day we could lean on people harder than you can now. That helped."

"Yeah but he has a way of getting people talking. It's uncanny. It's like he's a priest or something."

"Still, the gangsters aren't likely to spill too easily."

"Yeah, you're right. That's one of our biggest problems. That's why so many of their murders stay unsolved. But it somehow works out in the end. They have a kind of justice amongst their own."

"Now you're sounding like a salty, cynical cop I always knew you for."

He grinned and put the last bite of brat in his mouth. His phone rang and he picked it up.

"Roberts," he said. "Yeah...Good...We'll be waiting."

He hung up and looked at me.

"We hit the jackpot," he said. "McSpadden was picked up on a routine traffic stop. Gray and Villacorta have just taken him from the uniform. They also found the murder weapon in the glove box. Can you believe it?"

"I can, sometimes people have a helluva time throwing away their favorite toys."

We threw our garbage in a bin on the way up to homicide and Roberts grabbed his folder on McSpadden. I kept thinking if this was a waste or not. I figured it was. It's always a waste to kill a man. Okay, maybe not always, but most of the time. You never know when someone might make good with their life. It happens. I'm not that cynical yet. I can count on my one hand the number of really innocent people who have been murdered. Now that's the real shame.

We waited in Roberts' office while Villacorta and Gray gave McSpadden the tourists' tour of LA. At least that's what it felt like. I couldn't figure out why I was so impatient. I didn't have anything set up after this. I guess I just liked the last turn in the track when you close out the case. It always gave me a thrill.

I finished my soda and threw it Roberts' trash can for a three pointer when Villacorta and Gray brought McSpadden in. He was dressed in jeans and had on an open short sleeved shirt over a wife beater. He was handcuffed behind his back and he looked as miserable as the day I had first seen him.

Villacorta and Gray came by and saw us after they'd put him into the interview room. Gray held out the M1911A1 in a big baggie.

"The smoking gun," he said, grinning.

"That's great work," I said.

"Lady Luck more like it," said Villacorta. "He was heading out of town when he was stopped for speeding. Because we'd put a BOLO on him the uni did the right thing and called it in."

"Where was he headed?" asked Roberts.

"Hard to say," said Gray, "but looked like Las Vegas."

"The city of broken dreams and that two-faced mistress, Lady Luck," I said.

"Never won huh?" asked Villacorta, looking at me as if I'd just popped his helium balloon.

"I've given them more than I've taken," I said. "I only play poker now. At least then I can see who's getting rich off me."

"I want you guys to get that gun to ballistics and Anthony and I will interview old man McSpadden. By the way did he confess at all?"

Villacorta and Gray shook their heads.

"We told him he was under arrest for the murder of Hartley and we gave him his Miranda. All he said was 'okay'," said Gray.

"I think we can get it out of him," I said to Roberts as Gray and Villacorta left with the smoking gun.

"Let's go talk to McSpadden," said Roberts.

I followed him into the interrogation room and we sat down opposite the accused. Roberts put the closed folder down in front of him. McSpadden looked at it. He was still handcuffed at the back. He smelled as if he'd been bathing in a whisky barrel. His nose was even redder under the florescent lamps of the room, and in this harsh light his face was the color of sidewalks and just as pockmarked.

"You know why you're here?" asked Roberts, looking up at McSpadden.

McSpadden nodded but Roberts reminded him anyway.

"You're under arrest for murder. The murder of Hartley."

Roberts opened up the folder and took out a crime scenes' photo of the deceased. It was a headshot. The gunshot wound in the middle of his forehead looking surreal. If I hadn't known any better I might have suspected it of being faked. McSpadden looked at it nonchalantly. Then he looked back at Roberts.

"Did you do it?" asked Roberts.

McSpadden yawned and then shrugged his shoulders. He wasn't smug. He seemed like a tired old man all used up.

"Well, McSpadden," said Roberts. "We've got enough evidence here to convict you. I'm pretty sure of that."

Roberts shuffled some papers in the folder, taking his time to look at them. Then he turned his attention back on McSpadden.

"We've got the gun, which is headed to ballistics now. I'm pretty sure it's going to be a match with the slug found in Hartley's head. That gun is registered to you. Was your deceased son's but you got ownership of it when he died."

I was watching McSpadden as Roberts spoke. As he mentioned his son, life flickered at the back of McSpadden's eyes like a stoked fire. It was hot and angry.

"I see here, you've been swabbed for gunshot residue, and guess what. You're a winner there too. Not that we needed it, but it's nice of you to help us out with that. I'm pretty sure we're going to find your fingerprints on the gun too. All of what I've shared with you so far is enough to send you to jail for life. But wait, there's more."

Roberts took out a handful of papers from the folder and waved them about as if they were money and he was trying to catch the attention of a stripper at some strip joint.

"These are copies of your correspondence to the Army and Veterans' Affairs. You're practically threatening Major Hartley's - retired - life. Then we have video of you leaving the casino just after Hartley is escorted out. And here's you," said Roberts, putting his finger on an image of McSpadden entering the hotel, "entering the hotel shortly after Hartley."

Roberts put the papers back into the folder and closed it.

"Slam dunk. What I want to know is why?"

Roberts stared at McSpadden and the two of them locked horns for a while.

"You're the detective," said McSpadden at last, "you figure it out."

I figured now was my time. I had the sense McSpadden wanted to let go of the burden. Hell, maybe he even wanted to brag. I figured he just wanted a sympathetic ear. I could offer him that.

"I know what it's like," I said to him.

He looked at me skeptically.

"I lost a son recently in Afghanistan," I said, and I tried to choke on the words. I paused for effect, and I swallowed hard.

"Is that so?" he asked, without care or compassion.

I looked at him hard through lowered lids and slight frown.

"You mocking me?" I said, gritting my teeth. "You better not be mocking me about my son's service and sacrifice."

I started to get out of the chair like I meant it. McSpadden shook his head and leaned back a bit.

"No, sorry, I didn't mean it like that. I thought you were shitting me," he said.

I sat back down, and lowered my defenses.

"What kind of a man do you think I am? I know the pain. I wouldn't play something like that."

We looked at each other for a while and I could feel him searching inside my soul. It's a big, dark empty place sometimes and I can fill it with what I like. I gave him what he needed. He nodded at me.

"I'm sorry," he said.

"Not as sorry as I was. Unlike you, I had no one to blame it on. You see, my son was leading the fire team when they got ambushed and killed. Just a routine tour through the city when they were slaughtered like dogs."

I coughed and pretended to choke up on my words. I felt my eyes get a little wet. Perhaps I should've been an actor. I turned away to compose myself for a moment.

"Anyway," I said, when I continued, "it was all on him. My boy. He made a bad decision, he relaxed his guard and now I've got no son. And three other families have no sons, and one of them likes to let me know about it every month."

I looked down. My head hung heavy and weary with the guilt and shame of it all. Then I looked up at him again with a special, kind and soft look. Like we'd just been through a war together.

"Everyday I wish I had someone else to blame," I said. "I'd probably have done the same as you. I'd probably have killed the bastard if he'd put my son in that position."

We looked at each other for what seemed like minutes. Like we were the only two men in that room, tied together by a common thread of pain and loss.

"It was either gonna be me or him. And I didn't see how justice would be served if it was me."

McSpadden stopped to observe me. He was judging me to see how I was judging him. One of the benefits of being a humble PI is that I'm not a judge or jury, at least not when I'm interrogating the suspect. So I nodded at him slowly, knowingly, understandingly, and I held his gaze softly as if I'd captured a butterfly.

"Nobody had any remorse. Yeah, they said they were sorry but they didn't mean it. My son was just a number to them. And Hartley, that miserable son of a bitch. You know what he said to me when I put the gun to his face?"

I shook my head slowly and sympathetically.

"No," I said. "What did he say to you?"

"He said war was hard business. He said he'd lost dozens of men, many who were better than my son. Can you believe that?"

I shook my head and pinched my lips together. That was pretty cold.

"So I shot him. I shot him right in the fucking face that arrogant bastard. And I'm glad for it."

He looked at me then. His mouth was quivering and his eyes were welling up with tears. It hadn't gotten rid of his pain. And I knew it wouldn't have.

"It didn't kill the pain though," I said, "did it?"

He shook his head.

"No. Losing my boy cost me everything. My wife left me after I turned to drink. I had nothing but this big hot stone in my belly and I just wanted to get rid of it. I thought if I confronted Hartley that it would help. I thought he'd be genuinely sorry and remorseful and I could get on with my life. Or at least find my way back home. But he didn't..."

McSpadden stopped then for a moment and sobbed. I could feel the pain come up out of him, hot like lava and filling the room. I was moved. Genuinely.

"But he didn't," said McSpadden, looking down as tears dropped like shards of glass into his lap. "He said there were many better men than my son. He lied to me and he ridiculed my son's service. He had to pay."

I looked over at Roberts and he shook his head at me with disbelief. He stood up. I stood up next to him.

"Someone will come for you in a minute," he said.

McSpadden looked up at us as we turned to leave. I stopped by the door, and looked back at him.

"I'm sorry for your loss, really," I said, and I was. He nodded at me and I left, closing the door behind.

"I'd forgotten how good you were at lying to suspects," said Roberts, grinning at me like a proud papa.

"War," I said, "what is it good for?"

"Keeping us employed I suppose."

JASON BLACKER

"I'd rather sleep under the stars."

Washed Up

I was watching the beached whales trying to tan themselves on the Santa Monica Beach. I was sitting at the Chess Park smoking a cigarette and enjoying the midmorning sunshine on my face. Mornings and evenings were my favorite times of the day. The weather was cooler and the people sparser. It was late September and the weather could still get hot.

I watched a lazy Chinese man on a bicycle take his dog for a run. It was a small poodle, and I couldn't figure out if he was a genius or an idiot. The dog was working hard. He was barely pedaling. You get all sorts down here. For example, at a chess table a little ways away from me was a homeless man who looked like an older Jesus. He had gray hair and a scruffy beard. He was wearing tattered cargo pants, sandals and a black wife beater. He was playing chess by himself, and from what I could tell he was commenting on the results. Only he didn't play from one seat. No, he kept getting up and changing seats each time he wanted to play as the other player. Perhaps he was trying to give it more authenticity.

I didn't particularly care. I just liked the way the pier took my mind off things. I watched the roller coaster take a couple of tours along the pier and I couldn't figure out the attraction in that. If I wanted to move around I'd take a car and go someplace.

Staring at the pier and all the human ants crawling all over it like it was a sliver of cake left at the beach, I noticed a group gathering down at the tideline just under the pier. I watched it after a while. Every so often, something interesting would wash up and get caught up on the legs of the pier. I'd seen a dead shark once washed up under there. Crabs too, you could find quite a few crabs if you were careful.

But this looked different, I started to notice a few cops come on down and tape up the area. The yellow tape was what caught my eye and I became more interested in what was going on. I stubbed out my cigarette and got up, wishing old Jesus well with his chess match.

I strolled down to see what was what. The crowd was growing bigger now and more unis were blocking the view. I walked up to one and he put his hand out to stop me.

"What's going on?" I asked.

He looked at me as if I'd asked to date his sister. I walked along the crowd towards the water. I made it to the edge and took off my shoes and socks and rolled up my socks. I walked into the water up to my knees and across towards the pier. I could see what looked like a body lying slightly under the pier, but a couple of plain clothes were blocking the view.

"Sir! Sir!" came the shout of a wet behind the ears the cop. "I'm going to have to get you to move that way."

He was gesticulating with his hands to get me to head back from where I'd come. I smiled at him and ignored him. He was getting more worked up.

"Sir!" he yelled. "I'm serious. You've got to get back now. Goddamn!"

I kept going and he matched my pace but he stayed on they dry sand. One of the plain clothes looked up at me and grinned.

Then he nudged one of the others who was kneeling in front of him. This cop got up. He shook his head at me and smiled.

"It's alright," he said to the young uni. "He's with us. For Chrissakes, Anthony, can I get any work done by myself?"

It was Captain John Roberts. An old friend whom I'd taught everything I knew about crime fighting.

"You that desperate for work you're gonna swim ashore here to help me?"

"I just want to make sure you get a conviction," I said. "You know how helpless you are without me."

He shook his head.

"This is Detective Ashley Schaal and Detective Ray Campos."

Schaal was my height and about my build. She was an old school policewoman, butch looking in her mid-forties with short gray hair that she didn't bother coloring. I hadn't met her before. Campos was a slim, good looking Hispanic man who could have made more money as a model. He was also about my height, in his mid-thirties with wet, curly black hair. He was in dark blue pants and blue shirt with pink stripes. He wore it well. We didn't shake hands but they both nodded at me.

"You gonna put on your socks and shoes?" asked Roberts.

"Not until my feet are dry. What have you got here?"

Roberts turned to look down at the body. I came up next to him and had a look.

"Young guy," said Roberts, "looks like he was stabbed multiple times. He's soaking wet so he probably wasn't killed here. The tide's been going out all morning. Probably got washed up last night."

I looked down at the young boy. He looked like a teenager, but he might have been twenty, even twenty-one. He was a white man of about average height, but on the husky side of the scale. He wore a blue UCLA t-shirt and pale yellow board shorts. He had no shoes. I counted three stab marks to his lower abdomen.

They had been washed clean. There was no blood anywhere near him.

"No blood, no shoes, and he's looking pretty bloated. I reckon he's been washed up like you said," I acknowledged.

Schaal looked at me like I was an idiot repeating everything Roberts had just said.

"Why is he here?" she asked Roberts.

I liked her already. Roberts looked over at her and smiled.

"He'll be consulting with us. Don't let his aw shucks attitude fool you, he was the best homicide detective we've had in years."

She looked me up and down.

"If you say so," she added, speaking to Roberts.

"She's always like that," said Campos.

"I don't suppose we've got any ID, a name or anything?" I asked.

Roberts shook his head.

"John Doe for now, hopefully we'll get lucky with the prints."

I took out my phone and snapped a picture of his marble white, dead face. I put my phone back in my pocket.

"I'll be in touch this afternoon," I said to Roberts.

I walked away from them and ducked under the yellow tape. I heard Roberts tell them I was like that sometimes.

"What happened?" asked a tall college aged kid with dirty blonde hair.

"Somebody harpooned a whale," I said to him with a straight face. He frowned at me trying to figure it out. I walked off towards the chess park again to dry my feet and put on my shoes.

Washed Up: Chapter Two

UCLA is like a small, quaint town in the middle of LA. A place where kids transform from awkward teenagers into the captains and titans of industry. At least that's what I'm told. It's east of the 405 and sprawls on over 400 acres of prime LA real estate that's likely worth more than some small countries.

Though I reckon that if we the fault split, UCLA might end up like the fable city of Atlantis. As would I, but it's not something that keeps me up at night. What keeps me up at night is Pirate's claws on my jugular.

I parked in the parking lot by Murphy Hall which is where the Registrar's Office is located. It's on the far east side just off Hilgard Avenue. The parking lot had half a dozen spots left in it, and my 2000 LeSabre didn't seem too out of place.

I sat in the parking lot for a minute wondering if I'd thought this out properly. I figured that UCLA had to accept several thousands of students each year. How the hell were they going to recognize a student from just a photograph? I didn't have any idea now that I thought about it. But I was here and I might as well roll the dice. You don't always come up snake eyes. Hell even some pensioner's gotta win the slots once in a while, and I felt lucky.

I got out of my car and put on my fedora. I walked over the Registrar's Office like I knew where I was going. There were a few kids in the line in front of me. Probably trying to change courses. I waited a few minutes when I was called up front.

The woman behind the desk had a name tag that said "Darlene". It suited her well. She was an older woman with dyed brown hair and a thick schmeer of makeup. Even from across the desk, her rose-scented perfume would knock out a honey badger. I smiled at her and put on my serious cop face.

"I'm with the LAPD," I said, hoping she wouldn't ask for my badge, "and I need to speak with someone familiar with undergraduate admissions."

She looked me up and down and nodded at me. Then she got up and walked behind her to a field of open desks and behind them a few offices. She disappeared from my view for a few moments. When she came back she was followed by a middle-aged woman in a gray business suit over a pin-striped blouse. She had jet black hair that was cropped short around her face and she was trim and pretty. Darlene pointed to the end of the counter. I walked over to meet them. The woman in the business suit put out her hand and introduced herself to me. He skin was soft and her fingers slender.

"Linda Pacheco," she said, "I'm one of the undergraduate assistant registrars."

"Anthony Carrick," I said.

She opened up a swing door in the desk and invited me inside. I followed her away from the main desk to a small office in the back. After she sat down I took a seat across from her and her desk. I scooted up closer.

"So you're with the LAPD," she said.

I nodded.

"I'm helping them with a homicide," I said, smiling at her.

"So you're not actually a cop."

"No."

"Then I'm not sure how I can help you."

She was frowning icicles above her eyebrows and I wanted to thaw them off.

"Listen," I said, "just hear me out for a few minutes. What I'm asking for is a long shot. I'm not even sure the young man murdered goes to UCLA. Further, I don't even know his name. This is what we're trying to find out. All I've got is a picture."

She stared at me blankly as if I'd just spoken Xhosa.

"If this young man hasn't come into contact with law enforcement we won't have his prints. If we don't have his prints, it gets harder to find out who he is. And the longer we're taking trying to figure out his name the easier it is for the murderer to go unpunished. If we don't have a good handle on a suspect list in the first 48 hours, we might as well give the real killer a get out of jail free card."

I made that up, but I figured it couldn't hurt my case. After some time she nodded.

"You don't mind if I call LAPD," she said, "to verify your story."

She picked up the phone. I thought that was cute. She started dialing. I wasn't finding her all that cute anymore. I nodded my head anyway. I understood she had to be cautious.

"Ask for Captain John Roberts," I said.

I smiled at her and watched her dial. She wasn't calling any number associated with the LAPD that I was familiar with. I waited patiently. She looked at me long and hard while she had the phone to her ear. I smiled at her some more. Finally she put the phone down.

"You better not be lying to me," she said, as stern as a convent nun. I crossed my heart.

"Why would I lie about a homicide," I said.

She shrugged.

"Show me the picture of him."

I pulled out my phone.

"This was taken just this morning. Just so you know, he's dead, and a bit bloated from being in the ocean overnight."

She looked at me with her brown eyes, sweet as melted chocolate. She nodded again.

"I don't know if I'm going to be able to help you anyway," she said. "We get almost a hundred thousand applicants and we accept over fifteen thousand. I only know those personally who I've actually dealt with."

"I understand," I said. "I know this is a long shot, but it's better than nothing."

I pulled up the picture and turned my phone to her. She studied it for a moment, frowned and then brought her hand to her mouth. I smiled inside. I had beaten the Vegas odds on this one.

"Do you know him?"

She started to shake her head but stopped.

"It can't be," she said, "but it looks like Gregg Gelvan. Though I can't be sure."

She turned to her computer and typed on her keyboard for some time. Then she looked from her computer screen to my phone and back again.

"I think it is him," she said to me at last.

"Can I have a look?"

She pivoted the screen to me and I was staring at a smiling face. It was the deceased on my phone, only he had more color and he was smiling. I nodded solemnly.

"Yeah, looks like him," I said to her. "What's his name again.?"

She was staring at the picture on my phone. Mesmerized. I took it away and put it in my pocket.

"Sorry," she said. "I can't believe it."

"I asked for his name."

"Gregg Gelvan," she said without looking back at her screen. "What happened to him?"

I felt like I should offer up a morsel. She had done the same for me.

162

"It appears he was stabbed and most likely dumped in the ocean."

"I can't believe it, that's awful," she said.

"Well, I guess we're lucky that I happened upon you instead of someone else."

She nodded.

"I suppose so, but I just can't believe he's dead."

"So he was an honors student and came from a good family?"

I was being sincere. One murder in a hundred that might be the case, and this might be my hundredth case. Linda shook her head.

"No, quite the contrary but he was so easy going," she said to me.

"What do you mean quite the contrary?"

"He was an underdog, one of those kids you just can't help but root for. He came from Green Meadows, raised by a single mother but has no siblings."

"His father's out of the picture?"

"Yes, you know how it is."

I nodded.

"We've started an outreach program in South Los Angeles generally, in order to help more of those kids get into college and out of gangs. It's a partnership program with the city and the LAPD. We start at the junior high level and try and follow through to graduation. Gregg Gelvan was one of the pilot students we started with when we started the program at Locke High School."

I nodded at her. I hated these kinds of stories. Kid from the wrong side of the tracks does good, and then gets murdered.

"We offered a select group of these students a full ride at UCLA if they got a B average in Grade 12 and managed SAT scores of 550 or better in all three subjects. We were worried about Gregg because throughout high school he showed no inclination or determination to try and get a scholarship. Then in Grade 12 he really started pulling up his socks and just managed a B- overall. His SATs came in strong."

Linda pivoted the screen back to her and looked at it for a moment.

"He got over 600 in all three SAT subjects. He was really quite the turnaround story."

"600s on his SATs, that must put him fairly high up," I said.

Linda nodded.

"I'd have to look closer, but he'd probably be in the top 25 percent with those results."

That was quite the turnaround story.

"Anything specifically that prompted him to pull up his socks that you can think of?"

"His mother was diagnosed with quite aggressive breast cancer in the final months of Gregg's Grade 11. I think it affected him deeply. He wanted to study medicine."

I nodded. This was becoming a sadder story than I had imagined.

"Can you think of any arguments or disagreements with any other students that might have led to his murder?"

Linda shook her head.

"I'm afraid I can't help you there. Your best bet is to speak with one of our counselors. I believe that Vanessa Caraballo was in charge of his case from the very beginning. She'll likely have that sort of information."

"When can I see her?" I asked.

"Probably not without Captain Roberts. Our counselors take their client's confidentiality very seriously."

I nodded again, and started to feel like a bobblehead.

"Can you give me his address?"

"I will, but you'll have to be with a real cop," she said.

A "real" cop. I liked that. I had been a real cop and that's why I wasn't one anymore. Not to say they're all idiots, but the bureaucracy can sure blindfold you and tie you up tighter than a bondage mistress.

"Does he live on campus or is he commuting from Green Meadows?"

"His mother's cancer has become terminal in the last few months so she's in a hospice."

"Which one?"

"The Sisters of Mercy hospice in Green Meadows."

Linda looked at me.

"She was so proud of her son when they found out he'd won a scholarship to UCLA. I don't see how any good can come of telling her that her son has been murdered."

"No good can come of it at all. But the truth comes out whether we want it to or not."

"But she doesn't have much time left. I imagine it's only months."

"We'll be sensitive," I said, trying to reassure her. "So you're saying that Gregg lived on campus then?"

Linda nodded.

"Yes, we gave him campus shared housing considering his circumstances," she said. "It was the least he could do. So sad all of this. He was showing such promise."

I stood up and put my hand out for Linda to take. She stood up and shook it.

"I'll walk you out," she said.

"I'll be back with a real police officer," I said, putting a sarcastic tone on the "real". She smiled at that.

As I was leaving through the swinging door of the desk I had recently entered she asked me to get justice for Gregg. I told her I would. My mouth is a loose cannon like that.

I walked out to my car watching the vast number of young, bright-eyed faces coming and going to their classes with backpacks on their backs. The potential of the human race to improve itself. Or mow itself down prematurely. These scales of life and death were balanced precariously on the loose fulcrum of human foibles. I fished out my phone and called Roberts. He of all men might be happy to hear what I had found out.

Washed Up: Chapter Three

Roberts picked me up by the pier at a little before five in the afternoon. I had headed back down there and had a late lunch at a nearby restaurant. Crime Scenes had finished up with the scene as I wandered down there after lunch to think and look. I didn't find anything. The LAPD's Scientific Investigation Division, or SID as they're officially called, is thorough.

I figured the deeper I dug the more that would come to the surface. You had to be slow and persistent like a gold panner. There were always gold nuggets waiting to be discovered for the patient man.

I sat in Robert's police cruiser as he drove us back to UCLA to see Vanessa Caraballo. She was the counselor to Gregg, and probably other angsty teenagers.

"We got a hit on Gregg's prints," said Roberts, looking ahead as we drove through slow moving traffic.

"So he's known to you," I said.

"Yeah. Not the worst juvenile to come out of Green Meadows. He was picked up for shoplifting, and joyriding. No violent offenses, and no time served."

"Practically a choir boy then for that side of town."

Roberts nodded.

"Linda the registrar I spoke to earlier found his death quite upsetting. Said he was a real turnaround case, and he'd done well in his final year. UCLA has this pilot program where they reach out to the disenfranchised. Gelvan was one of the first in the program at Locke High School. Didn't do anything for grade ten and eleven, but squeaked out a B average for grade twelve. Managed better on his SATs getting 600s in all three subjects."

"So you're saying that overnight he goes from joyriding, and failing classes to turning his whole life around?" asked Roberts not looking at me.

"Yeah, that's what I'm saying. These things happen. You're sounding as cynical as I usually am."

"Well I'm just saying, it seems pretty weird he suddenly decides he wants a better life."

"But I haven't told you the best part," I said. "He has a reason."

"Yeah, what's that?"

"His mother was diagnosed with terminal breast cancer sometime when he was finishing up grade twelve. Apparently something like that can motivate you."

Roberts nodded his head back and forth weighing the idea.

"Yeah, I suppose I can see that," he said.

We finally got past the San Diego Freeway and headed north on Westwood Boulevard. On Westwood the traffic was easy going, most of it was coming south as professors and students were leaving for the day. We parked in the parking lot close to Murphy Hall and managed to find our way to the counselors' offices after asking a fresh-faced blonde woman who talked like the rest of the bimbos from the valley.

The main window looked like it was closed but a woman in one of the back offices noticed us and came out to greet us. She was Vanessa Caraballo and she looked like a student. She had curly black hair that fell to her shoulders and a smile that you could tan under. She was average looking with unblemished brown skin wearing faded blue jeans and a UCLA t-shirt. The girl's version of what Gelvan had on him when he was a beached whale.

We followed her back to her office which was small but private. She closed the door behind us and sat down in an armchair in front of her desk. We took the soft couch that was in front of her. Her room had several plush toys placed about it and on her bookshelf were books on psychology and philosophy as well as board games.

"Thank you for seeing us," said Roberts.

"It's my pleasure," she said, sitting with her one leg crossed over her other and her hands clasped in her lap. She was slim and charming, giving off a nonjudgmental air. I could tell she was good at her job. She had introduced herself as Vanessa Caraballo and I was wondering if she was a doctor of psychology, so I asked.

"No," she said. "I just finished my masters in counseling two years ago and decided I'd get some work experience while I pursued my doctorate."

I nodded at her. She appeared to be an open book, but I doubted that was the case. What she did share, she shared freely.

"I heard that Gregg was stabbed multiple times," she said. "That's just awful."

"That's why we're here," said Roberts. "We need your help in trying to understand how and why this might have happened to him."

"Of course," she said. "Anything I can do."

"We understand that you were Gregg's counselor."

"That's right."

"Had you noticed any difference in his behavior lately? Anything that might have given you pause?"

Caraballo thought for a moment. She looked off to the ceiling and then shook her head.

"Nothing really. Though he did have quite a lot to deal with. He was generally a very easy going low key guy."

"What were some of the things he was dealing with?"

"As you've probably heard, his mother is dying from terminal breast cancer. The last I heard, that was weighing on him quite a bit. He told me that his mother most likely wouldn't see Christmas."

"When was the last time you saw him?"

"Last Friday, the twentieth I think it was."

"Can you tell us what you spoke about?"

"The usual things, though he seemed quite upset about not having found a job yet which I found unusual."

"Why was that?"

"Well, Gregg has a full ride here at UCLA. We encourage them to find work over the summer months but it's certainly not encouraged or necessary during the semester. Our scholarship students aren't required to work or contribute financially to their studies. So when Gregg seemed quite upset about not finding work I asked him why. He said he could really use the money. When I asked him what for he told me so he could just enjoy his free time a bit more. But I had the impression that he was lying."

"How so?"

"I can't put my finger on it, but when you've been counseling for a while you learn to trust your instincts and you learn to read people. Especially those you get to know. And I could just tell he wasn't being as forthcoming with me as he usually is. But I didn't push. I knew he'd come around when he was ready."

"He never gave you any reason to believe he was in trouble?" I asked.

Caraballo looked at me and smiled, slowly shaking her head.

"Listen, you have to understand. Kids from that neck of the woods are carrying around a lot of weight and baggage. Understandably so, they're often poor and come from a single parent household. Gregg was no different, but he had an easygoing manner. He was quite well adjusted all things considering."

"And how long had you know him?" asked Roberts.

"I got his case just after I finished up my masters. That's one of the reasons I chose to defer my doctorate. I thought this was a great program and I wanted to a be a part of it."

"So you've seen him through grade eleven all the way to acceptance here?" I asked.

She nodded.

"Yes."

"And you've seen no problems or behavioral issues since that time?"

"Well, not exactly. These aren't your kids from Bel Air and Beverly Hills. They have their problems."

I nodded quickly. I was getting the impression that I was getting the run around.

"I understand that Vanessa," I said. "I'm asking specifically about Gregg. We're trying to solve his murder and we need your help. We want to understand his quick turnaround from no chance of getting into UCLA in grade eleven to his B- in grade twelve and his great results on his SATs."

"You're right, Anthony. In grade eleven I thought we might lose him. He wasn't paying any attention at school, but he wasn't really getting into a lot of trouble either. He just didn't seem motivated. But then his mother got cancer as I said before, and everything changed for him. He wanted to study medicine so he could help his mother. That's what he said to me. Sometimes these kids just need a little bit of motivation, and I think his mother's cancer was that motivation."

"How well did you know him?" I asked.

"Well enough. Each of us has ten kids to help through this pilot project on top of being available to the regular student body at large."

"Did he visit you here or did you go out and see him when he was in high school?"

"We're always available to them, but generally we have to keep in contact. I visit each of my pilot students on a monthly basis and I touch base with them by phone on a weekly basis."

"And what about the peer group," said Roberts. "Do you have a chance to get to know these kids' friends and extended families and such?"

"Not as much as we'd like, at least not with their peer group. These kids are trying to cut the cord of poverty that often runs deep. There is genuine pressure from their peers that they don't get left behind, so most of these kids compartmentalize the side of them that is trying to get into college from their social circle. It's terribly hard for them. So to answer your question, no, we don't get a chance to interact with their friends to any great extent. We usually have a better rapport with the families and the extended families. In Gregg's case this was his mother. She was terribly proud when he got accepted. Most of her family she ceased contact with when she got out here. They're from the Midwest, and I'm sure there's a story there but I don't know what it is. Gregg's father has never been in his life either."

"Did he ever mention a girlfriend?" asked Roberts.

"Yes, that was an ongoing conversation with us. He had broken up with his girlfriend a few months ago and she hadn't taken it well. She's from Green Meadows too."

"What's her name?"

"Zaira Estrada," she said. "Her brothers are involved with the gang Trece Noches."

"How do you know that?"

"Gregg told me."

I looked at Roberts and he looked at me back.

"That's not a good sign, is it?" she asked.

"Not particularly," I said. "Was he worried about any retaliation?"

"That's hard to say. He had told me that her brothers had told him that if he ever hurt her they'd kill him, but he said that's how they talk in his neighborhood. I had the sense that he was mostly conflicted about how he felt. He was seeing someone else on campus. Her name is Stephanie Eastman."

"Where's she from?"

"Not sure, I'd have to check, but definitely not from his neighborhood."

"You said he was conflicted. Did he tell you any more about that?" asked Roberts.

"Yes. He was torn about how he felt. He told me he still loved Zaira. They had been dating since grade ten. He told me he was thinking about getting back together with her."

"Was that because he felt threatened or because he wanted to?" I asked.

"I believe it was what he wanted."

"Can you think of a reason for a person who might have wanted Gregg dead?" I asked.

Vanessa looked at me and nodded.

"I could think of several reasons, but none of them seem to be a valid reason to kill anyone."

"Try some on me," I said.

"Maybe he was murdered by one of his old friends who became disgruntled because Gregg's life is improving while theirs stays trapped. Perhaps Zaira's brothers killed him because he hurt her when he broke up with her. Maybe Stephanie found out he was thinking of getting back with his ex and she killed him. Or, maybe he was just at the wrong place at the wrong time. All of these by the way are just suppositions. I have no evidence for any of them."

I nodded. Any of those reasons were good enough for some people to kill someone. In my time I'd seen people murdered for less.

"Gregg was wearing the same blue UCLA t-shirt that you're wearing. Do you know how he came by it?" I asked.

"I gave it to him. I've given all the students from this program a t-shirt just like it. I find it helps keep them motivated. I give it to them when they're in grade twelve usually. You'll be amazed at how just a simple memento like that can feed their dreams and help them stay focused and determined."

I looked over at Roberts. I couldn't think of any other questions to ask. As usual, the early part of this investigation was filled with more questions than answers. Roberts looked over at me and then at Vanessa.

"Thanks for your help," he said, offering her his card which she took. "If you can think of anything, please give me a call."

We stood up and Vanessa shook our hands, and we started to leave, when I turned around to her.

"I just had a thought," I said. "Where can we find Stephanie?"

"She lives with her parents. I'll forward her address to you," she said, looking at Roberts.

We left her and made our way back to the car. Just before we got in, Roberts turned to me.

"You know the Trece Noches have killed over less," he said.

"True, but I'm skeptical. I want to find out why he needed a job so urgently."

"Maybe because he wanted to go out on better dates," said Roberts.

"Right," I said, and climbed into the passenger seat.

Washed Up: Chapter Four

East 109th Place is a rundown street a couple of blocks away from Locke High School in Green Meadows. How do I know this? Because Roberts and I had just arrived to pay a friendly visit to Zaira Estrada.

Most of the houses along this street like most of Green Meadows are rundown bungalows with metal arrowed fences and brown grass. Trees were sparse and the driveways were cracked and stained with oil. The stucco on the Estrada house was peeling and cracked and the window trim needed more than a coat of paint. This wasn't the kind of place that shouted pride of ownership. In fact the only thing that seemed to have been shown some tenderness was a pimped out late 80s Cadillac de Ville that sat in the drive.

As we drove up the driveway I noticed a "Beware of Dog" sign. Perhaps what it should have read was "Beware of God". The fear of God might have encouraged some of these folks to work for a living instead of looting and killing. The same sign was stuck to a window by the door. The door was open but the metal mesh security door which also needed a coat of paint was locked.

Roberts banged on the screen door and waited. I turned around and looked up and down the street. It was quiet. Maybe most of these people were actually working. Across the road an infill was being built. In some places it would fetch half a million, here it looked out of place like a Jehovah's witness.

"What you want," said a short fat and bald Hispanic wearing a white vest and the requisite tattoos of Trece Noches.

Roberts pointed at his police badge stuck to the right side of his pants.

"I'm John Roberts and I need to speak with Zaira Estrada about Gregg Gelvan."

The Hispanic took a swig from the can of beer he was holding.

"You got the wrong house."

"I've got the right house," said Roberts.

"Well, she don't want to talk to the cops."

"Let me hear it from her."

"Unless you got a warrant, I ain't gonna talk to you."

Roberts fished out a card and handed it through a slit in the metal door.

"Ask her to call me," he said.

"Yeah, I'll do that," said the Hispanic sarcastically as he walked away.

I could see straight through the house to the back door past the kitchen. I couldn't see any weapons visible in the house and I couldn't see or hear a dog. Roberts stepped off the porch and started to walk down the driveway.

"What are you doing?" I asked.

"Anthony, I don't have a warrant and unless we have some evidence or a warrant I can't just force myself into his house, as much as I'd like to."

I put my hand up to my ear.

"Do you hear that?" I asked him.

"What?"

"Someone's crying for help from inside," I said.

"Bullshit," he said, shaking his head at me. "Listen, if we want to catch the killer we have to play by the rules."

"You have to play by the rules," I said. "Just give me a minute, let me see if I can't reason with the guy."

"No, Anthony, that's not a good idea."

"Listen, you know me. I can be charming when I want to."

I left him to think about it for a minute as I walked around to the back of the house. These gangsters aren't always that smart. Take for instance the back of their house. Now most houses I know have a front door and a back door. Most times these gang bangers don't install a metal security door on the back. Don't ask me why. Maybe they're just frugal like that.

And the Estrada's place was no different. Even better, the back door was open. It was getting warm this morning. So I walked in. Now I know that's technically breaking and entering but I figured these guys wouldn't mind.

Two Hispanics were sitting at a small kitchen table. The fat one was facing me as I walked in. He had a cigarette in his mouth. I noticed by the kitchen sink there was a gun. I skipped in to stand between him and his gun. The other Hispanic who was thin but otherwise dressed the same with the same haircut now saw me.

"What the fuck, man!" said the fat Hispanic.

He got up, taking his time like he was going to show me out again. As soon as he stood up I planted a punch right on his soft nose. It sat him back down again, as the blood started pouring out.

"You mother fucker," said the thin Hispanic.

He was much faster than the fat one, he came at me quickly but I sidestepped him and used his momentum to ram his face into the corner of the kitchen counter. It got him right on the bridge of the nose. He dropped like a sad sweaty sack of rotten apples. I left him there to bleed on the floor. I picked up the gun that was by the sink and put it in my pocket.

"My partner asked if he could speak with Zaira," I said. "Are you gonna let him?"

"You cops can't just break into my place," said the fat Hispanic as he sat wiping blood onto his forearm.

"I'm not the cops," I said.

"Then what the fuck do you want?"

"I want you to stop cursing and let my partner in so we can talk to Zaira. That's all we want to do. Just talk to her."

I heard footsteps running down the hall to the front door. That had to be Zaira. I turned to follow her down the hall, as I got there she was just exiting the metal security door and running straight into Robert's arms.

"See," I said to him, "they want you to come inside."

Roberts grabbed Zaira by the arm and pulled her into the house. She was yelling and screaming and telling him to let go of her.

"I'm a cop," he said, "and I just want to talk to you about Gregg."

He pushed her down onto the couch as I went into the kitchen to see what was what with my two new friends. The fat Hispanic had decided to grab a steak knife and made a thrust for me. I dodged out of the way and grabbed a wooden cutting board off the drying rack just as he came back at me with the knife again. I slammed the board down hard against his wrist hoping to break it. He dropped the knife and yelled in pain. As he reached for his limp hand with his good one and brought it towards his chest and I smacked him up the side of the head as hard as I could with the cutting board. He dropped as if I'd cut his legs out from under him.

I picked up the steak knife and put it in my pocket. I helped the thin Hispanic up.

"Are you gonna behave now?" I asked him. "We just want to ask Zaira a couple of questions.

He nodded at me through watery eyes and a swollen bleeding nose.

"Good," I said, "then grab your brother and drag him into the other room. I want to keep my eyes on you."

He did as he was told. I put the wooden board back down and put the knife into the sink. I grabbed the roll of paper towels and followed them out as he dribbled blood on the floor like rose petals as he dragged the fat one into the living room.

Roberts watched us as we came in. He was sitting on the couch next to Zaira.

"What have you done to Pampy," she said, and she started to punch Roberts on the shoulder and chest.

He had to restrain her until she settled down. Then he let her go. He looked at me and shook his head like a disapproving father. It didn't bother me. I knew deep inside he was grateful for my help. I gave the thin Hispanic the roll of paper towels. He took a couple of sheets and dabbed carefully at his nose as he sat down in a chair opposite the couch. The fat one started to get up too and touched the side of his head gingerly.

I pointed at the other chair next to the thin one. He sat in it and took a couple of paper towels from it and started to wipe his nose.

"Now that we're all here," I said, looking around the room, "I'm gonna assume that you're Zaira Estrada." I looked at her and she nodded carefully. Then I turned to the fat one.

"You must be Pampín Estrada." He nodded. "Which makes you Ezra Estrada," I said looking at the thin one. He nodded too. "Good. Now I want everyone to behave. We only want to ask some questions. Comprender?"

I looked around at everyone and they all nodded. I stood close to the door but halfway between the couch and Pampín.

"Fire away, John," I said.

John looked at Zaira.

"I want to ask you about Gregg Gelvan," he said.

"What about him?"

"He was murdered," said Roberts. "A couple of days ago."

Zaira furrowed her eyebrows and shook her head.

"No," she said, "that can't be."

She seemed upset but she wasn't a cloud of tears.

"What happened?" she asked.

"He was stabbed," said Roberts.

"Why?"

"That's what we're trying to find out."

"You and he dated for a while."

Zaira nodded her head.

"We met in grade ten and we dated until a few months ago."

"What happened?" asked Roberts.

"He told me he had started seeing someone new."

"That must have pissed you off."

"I know where you're going with this. I love him, okay, I didn't kill him."

"I didn't ask you that," said Roberts.

"But you might have," I said, looking at Tweedledee and Tweedledum.

"Nah man, you've got to be crazy, why'd we kill Gregg?" asked Pampín.

"Because you threatened to kill him if he hurt your sister. And he hurt your sister."

"Where'd you hear that?" he asked.

"From Gregg himself."

"Nah man, that was just crazy talk, you know. We were just looking out for our sister. Brothers say shit like that. Don't mean we meant it."

"They didn't do it," said Zaira. "It's just like Pampy said. They were only trying to protect me. Besides he didn't really hurt me. He never beat me or nothing."

"When did you see him last?" asked Roberts.

"Last weekend, he said he wanted to get back together with me. He said he was tired of that high maintenance bitch taking up all his time and what little money he had."

"You mean the woman he had been seeing."

"Yeah."

"When on the weekend did you see him?"

"He came by on Saturday evening. Pampy and Ezzy were here."

I looked at them and they nodded.

"That's a convenient alibi," I said, "but its not even big enough to be a spittoon."

Zaira shook her head and squinted at me. She had no idea what I meant.

"Did you hear him saying he wanted to get back with your sister?" I asked Tweedledee and Tweedledum.

Pampín shook his head.

"Nah man, they were in Zay's room. But when he left Zay seemed pretty happy. She told us they were going to get back together."

"And you didn't see him since then?" I asked.

Zaira shook her head. I looked at her two brothers. They shook their heads too. Pampín and Ezra had clumped soggy balls of pink paper towels in their laps. If those balls were any bigger I might have confused them for cheerleader's pompoms.

"You knew Gregg well. You're from the same neighborhood. Can you think of anyone who might have wanted to hurt him?" asked Roberts.

Zaira shook her head vigorously.

"No, everybody liked him. I mean sure, there were a couple of the students that got pissed because they didn't have the chance he had been given. But they wouldn't have killed him over it."

Pampín looked at his sister and raised his eyebrows at her. He thought he was being discreet. But when you've played poker awhile you can see a novice tell this side of the river.

"What?" I asked.

181

"Nothing," said Pampín looking down at his soggy ball of paper towels.

"We came here for a civilized, honest chat, and now you're holding out on us. If that's how it's gonna be, we'll take you downtown to think about it."

Pampín looked up at his sister and nodded at her carefully, slowly, like he had a big pain in the back of his neck. Zaira looked over at Roberts. Everyone was ignoring me. That was fine, I wasn't looking to make any friends around here.

"Tell us," encouraged Roberts.

"Well, I suppose it doesn't matter now," she said. "I mean Gregg's dead. But he shouldn't have gotten into UCLA."

"What do you mean?" asked Roberts.

"He cheated," she said. "After his mother got cancer he really wanted to get into UCLA to make her proud. But he had ADD or something and he wasn't good at studying. So with the help of me and my brothers he cheated."

"How did he cheat?"

"We knew a guy who could get access to the final grade twelve exams and so he gave Gregg the answers. If you look at his grades up until the final exams you'll see he was getting like Cs and Ds. Then in the finals he got high Bs and low As."

"This guy also found someone who could take the SATs for Gregg with fake ID."

"And you think this guy wanted to kill Gregg?" asked Roberts.

"I don't know. All I know is that this whole thing cost ten grand. Ten grand that Gregg didn't have. He was nervous about it. He told me this guy kept hounding him for the money and threatening him if he didn't pay up by the time school started."

"Does this guy have a name?"

"Dennis Evans," said Zaira.

She looked nervously over at her brothers. Pampín nodded at her again.

"What's that about?" I asked.

Pampín looked at me.

"She's worried about ratting out on Dennis. But we can take care of her if he tries anything."

"Nice of you," I said sarcastically.

"You three stick around," said Roberts standing up from the couch. "I might need to talk to you again. Next time, just let me in nice and easy."

He looked at Pampín hard, like he thought he was Uri Geller. Pampín bent his head down in acknowledgement. I needed to ask Roberts how he did that.

"You've got my card. Use it if you think of anything else," said Roberts.

We walked out of the house and down the driveway where we crossed the road and stopped by the car. It was going to be a warm day. I took out Pampín's gun and handed it to Roberts.

"I doubt this is registered," I said.

"You're psychic," he replied, grinning at me.

"Where to next?"

"I want to visit the other love of Gregg's life. See if she's got any light to shed on this."

We got into the car and Roberts called UCLA. Stephanie Eastman was in class until noon. They said they'd call her to the counselors' offices and at that time we could interview.

Washed Up: Chapter Five

We parked in the same black scorched piece of tarmac we had the day before when we visited the counselor. I was starting to feel like a senior about to graduate. I wondered if I could choose my degree. We walked up towards the building as the unrepentant vigor of youth leered at us with their perky bosoms, six pack abs and smooth as pudding skin.

"Did you visit his mother yet?" I asked as we walked towards the entrance.

He looked at me and grinned.

"I sent Schaal and Campos yesterday afternoon."

"You cowardly bastard," I said to him.

"Hey, that's the perks of being the Captain of homicide. What would you have done?"

"Exact same thing," I said grinning.

"There you go."

At the main desk in the counselors' reception area, Roberts introduced himself again and showed his badge. The receptionist left her desk and disappeared. She came back out with Vanessa. I wasn't surprised about that.

"Hello again," she said, greeting us as she led us into the main area and towards her desk. "I wish it was under better circumstances."

"Agreed," I said, though in truth I enjoyed any reason to see her.

Vanessa let us in to her office, where Stephanie was seated on the couch. We stood in front of her as Vanessa went and got a chair. I took it from her and sat down in it. Vanessa sat in her easy chair close to the sofa and Roberts sat down on the couch next to Stephanie.

Stephanie was a plain looking woman with thin lips and a pudgy face. She had dirty blonde hair that dropped to her shoulders and overall she was soft and pillowy. A slimmer version of the Michelin man, but by no means to be mistaken for the svelteness of a model. On the desk in front of the couch a half empty box of tissues was available. Stephanie had been making good use of them.

Her eyes were swollen and red rimmed. She had been crying. A clump of crumpled origami tissue balls were lying on the desk within reach of her and she clutched a damp one in her hand.

"I take it you've heard about Gregg," said Roberts in his caring uncle's voice.

Stephanie nodded.

"Just to be certain," he said, "you are Stephanie Eastman?"

She nodded her head again and her hair barely moved.

"Can you tell me when the last time was that you saw Gregg?"

"On Tuesday night. Am I in trouble?"

"Not unless you killed him," said Roberts.

Stephanie choked and shook her head.

"God no, I loved him."

Then she took to crying again and we all waited until she had composed herself.

"I know this is difficult," said Roberts. "But you might be able to help us determine who killed him. That's why we need to ask you some questions, okay?"

He picked up the box of tissues and offered it to her. She pulled out two of them, and gave him a limp smile. She nodded her head again.

"I want to help," she said.

"That's good," said Roberts. "Where did you see Gregg on Tuesday night and what time was it?"

"I saw him in my room. He came to visit me to tell me that everything was going to be alright. It was around ten when he came by."

"What did he mean by everything was going to be alright?"

"Well, about a week before he seemed distant and upset. I asked him what was wrong and he said that he wasn't sure he could be with me. He said he felt bad about leaving all his friends behind while he went on to have a better chance. I think he felt guilty, and I also think he hadn't gotten over Zaira."

"So you know about her?"

"Yes, but I've never met her. Gregg was pretty careful about keeping his two worlds separate."

"Carry on," said Roberts, nodding at her encouragingly.

"Well, he said he needed a break from us. I was devastated."

"When was this?"

"The weekend before this one just gone."

"Go on."

"So for about that next week I didn't see him. We don't have the same classes or anything. But then on Saturday I found out I was pregnant. I told him on Sunday, and he seemed pleased. But he said he had to sort a couple of things out first. I didn't see him until Tuesday night like I said."

"And what happened?"

"He said everything was going to be alright. He said me getting pregnant had helped him understand what he really wanted. And he wanted a family with me. He wanted to tell his mother she was going to be a grandmother. I asked him about Zaira, and he said that she'd have to understand. His past was behind him now and he needed to take care of the future with us."

"You and your baby?"

She nodded.

"I'd never seen him so happy," she said. "But he said there was just one thing left he had to take care of. He said he had to see this guy about something first."

"What did he mean by that?" asked Roberts.

"I don't know. But he left me just before midnight. He told me not to worry, that after he'd finished this last thing we could just focus on our future together. He said he was going to get a job and take care of me and the baby."

"Did he tell you where he was going?"

"He said he was meeting this guy at the pier. I told him the pier was closed, but he said it would be alright."

"And he didn't tell you anything about who he was meeting or why he was meeting this guy."

"No. I pressed him for information but all he said is it had to do with his past, and that this was the last loose end. He told me not to worry about it... God, do you think that might have been who killed him?" she sobbed.

"We don't know at the moment," said Roberts. "We're still trying to run down all the leads we have."

"Maybe if I'd just been more determined not to let him go, he'd still be alive," she said, sobbing into her tissue.

"I wouldn't blame yourself," said Roberts. "It's not your fault."

"No, it isn't Steph. You can't beat yourself up about it," said Vanessa.

I just sat there like a mute at a Dale Carnegie conference. Friendless and without influence.

"I miss him," said Stephanie, "and now I have his baby and she'll never know her father."

"She?" asked Roberts.

"Gregg wanted a girl, but of course it's too early to tell the sex."

Stephanie put on a brave face that kept slipping off like molten wax.

"I have to ask a very difficult question," said Roberts, "of both of you."

He looked from Stephanie to Vanessa. Vanessa frowned at him and Stephanie looked startled.

"Did either of you know that Gregg had cheated on his SATs and his grade twelve finals?"

"No, he didn't. That can't be," said Stephanie. "He worked so hard."

"That can't be right," said Vanessa.

"We have heard that Gregg owed ten grand to a guy who got him the answers to the grade twelve finals and had someone take his SATs for him," said Roberts.

"That's impossible," said Vanessa.

"Not impossible, just not something we'd usually consider. But desperation will drive some to all sorts of nefarious lengths."

"Really?" asked Vanessa.

Behind her professional veneer the wallpaper was peeling showing the mold underneath.

"We haven't had it confirmed yet, but we'll be speaking with the alleged contributor to this problem later. Looking past your feelings for Gregg, can you see how this might be even remotely possible?" asked Roberts.

Vanessa put her index finger to her lip and looked up at the ceiling for a moment.

"Yes, I suppose it could be possible," she said.

"Right," said Roberts, "because he was struggling all through grade eleven and grade twelve. Then suddenly with his finals he manages to squeak in with a B-, and his SAT scores are really more like a high B or even A student's scores, wouldn't you say?'

"Yes, that's right. I'd hate to believe it though. He was such a good kid really. I really thought he was going to be one of the true turnaround stories of this pilot project. A beacon of hope for others so that we might expand it. You have to understand, Captain, I really thought ever since he found out about his mother's cancer that he had changed and started taking his studies seriously. I still think he might have made us proud, if he'd had a chance to get started this term."

"I understand how you feel," I said, trying to add something to this three sided conversation. "It doesn't sound like he was maliciously trying to fool you or the university. Perhaps he would have managed better in the university setting. Many kids if they find a way in often perform better than their grades in high school might have suggested they would."

"You're quite right, Mr. Carrick. As a counselor here I've often seen that. Not all the time but often enough that it keeps you encouraged and motivated to help the later bloomers as we call them."

Roberts looked over at Stephanie who had managed to take control of her emotions.

"I have to ask you this," said Robert, "but what did you do after Gregg left?"

"If you're asking if I have an alibi, I don't. I went to bed. Happily too, I might add. I really believed that things were turning for the better for us when he left, after the conversation we had had."

"Do you live in shared accommodation or do you have a private room?"

"I have a private room."

Roberts nodded. He fished into his pant's pocket and pulled out a couple of business cards. He handed one to Stephanie and one to Vanessa.

"I don't think I have any more questions at the moment."

He paused for a few seconds and looked from one to the other.

"Is there anything you'd like to add?"

He waited. Stephanie shook her head.

"I don't think so, Captain," said Vanessa, "this has come as quite an awful shock. Very unexpected. I hope you'll get justice for Gregg. He was a good man."

Roberts nodded and stood up. I stood up with him.

"That is my goal," he said.

Vanessa stood up and turned to Stephanie.

"I'll just show them out and then I'll be right back."

Stephanie nodded.

"I'm sorry for your loss," said Roberts, looking Stephanie in the eye for a couple of seconds. He was good at that sort of thing.

Then he turned around and we followed Vanessa out.

"Please keep me posted," she said as we shook hands goodbye.

When we got to the car John asked me where I wanted to go.

"Some place where the servers are buxom and the steaks are thick. I'm starving," I said.

"I think I'll join you," he said. "I know just the place."

Washed Up: Chapter Six

Roberts had dropped me off at around two thirty in the afternoon. I had enjoyed two beers at the restaurant he'd taken me too. One for me and one for him that I had to enjoy because he was on duty. He hadn't lied to me. The steaks were as thick as my wrist and women were buxom. It was a place called Carl's Ranch in Playa del Rey.

I'd spent the afternoon in my stuffy apartment with Pirate purring on my lap and me nodding off intermittently watching steroid junkies getting paid way too much to throw a ball around and hit it with a piece of dead wood.

The call came in during the ninth inning and I was glad for it. Other than baseball my best bet was an afternoon talk show. I figured it was a toss-up between a kick in the nuts or a kick in the ass. Though the more I thought about it the more I decided I was going to head down the beach and sketch half-naked women. But then Johnny called.

He told me that Schaal and Campos had picked up Dennis Evans, the guardian angel to helpless students. If they have the cheddar. Roberts said they were bringing him in but that he wasn't in a good mood. Schaal had tasered him for disregarding her instructions. I smiled at that. I figured that Schaal would have used the smallest opportunity to use force even when unnecessary. I'd worked with cops like her before. Always looking to escalate rather than deescalate a situation.

I got into my car and drove downtown to headquarters. It was always a hassle to visit there, but I put up with it considering LAPD was paying me two fifty a day to help out. I got my visitor's pass and clearance to head up to homicide.

When I got there, Roberts was waiting in his office. I walked in like I owned the place. I had once.

"What are you grinning you at?" he asked me, looking up to see the big smile on my face.

"I'm thinking Schaal is going to cause you problems in the future," I said.

"How so."

"I reckon she's got a hair trigger. Am I right?"

Roberts nodded slowly.

"That's one of the reasons she's in homicide. The less she has to do with the general public the less reprimands she gets."

"So that's how this place is run nowadays. Problems are promoted. It's the Peter Principle at work."

Roberts shook his head at me.

"No, that's not how it works. But she's a good detective, she's put in over twenty years with the department. She earned her promotion."

I nodded.

"Keep telling yourself that, until she gets your ass hauled upstairs to the Chief's office."

"Oh, ye of little faith. That's already happened twice. Once more and she's on riding desk."

We both laughed.

"Today might be your lucky day then," I said. "By the way where is the man who offers a helping hand to wayward students."

"He's just getting checked out by the medic. He should be back here any minute where you and I can play good cop with him."

"You mean good cop bad cop?"

"No, I mean good cop good cop. Schaal's done enough bad cop for the both of us."

I smiled and nodded at him and took a seat across from his desk.

"Do you have any further info from the good proctologist?" I asked.

"You mean the coroner. Yes. He puts TOD at between midnight and two a.m. Says he bled out quite quickly. One of the kidneys was nicked by the knife."

"What kind of a knife?"

"Your standard folding pocket knife with about a three and a half inch blade. Plain blade, not serrated."

Roberts looked up through the windowed partitions of his office. He nodded out towards the hallway.

"They're bringing him in now," he said.

I got up and turned around. Schaal and Campos were guiding a big black man into the interview room.

"Let's solve a murder," said Roberts.

"Always the optimist," I said.

I followed Roberts into the interview room. Just as we got there Schaal and Campos came out.

"Everything good?" Roberts asked.

Schaal nodded. Campos smiled.

"He didn't go down too quick," he said. "Schaal had to squeeze on the juice."

"I'm not gonna hear about this, am I?" Roberts asked looking at Schaal.

"No Captain, it was a good use of force," she said.

"Is that so?"

Roberts looked at Campos and he shrugged and tossed his head to the side.

"I didn't really see what happened," he said. "We had split up."

"And that's what you're gonna tell IA?"

"It was good, Captain. Besides, he ain't gonna complain, we have an understanding."

"Good."

Inside the interview room Dennis Evans was seated away from the door behind a metal table that was bolted to the floor. He was wearing a pair of silver handcuffs in front of him and his hands were in his lap.

It looked to me like he spent too much time in the gym with juice. He was well muscled under the black wife beater. On his head he wore a black bandana with white skull and crossbones. He had a well groomed goatee and a diamond in each ear. He wore camo-colored cargo shorts and hiking boots.

He looked up at us sideways with a smirk.

"That bitch is off the chain, man. I wanna make a citizens' complaint about excessive force."

"Is that right?" asked Roberts.

"Damn right."

"Looks to me like you're on the wrong side of the table to be asking questions," said Roberts. Roberts opened up a folder that he had brought in. "It says here you were threatening officers Schaal and Campos with a knife when they came to pick you up."

"Man, that's bullshit. It ain't like that. I was eating an apple that I had cut up. The knife was on the table by the plate. I stood up and that bitch just goes zapping me with the taser. Doesn't even give me a warning."

"They also found an ounce of marijuana on you too."

"Nah man, that wasn't on me, it was on the table by my apple."

"You had the munchies," I said, smiling.

He looked at me, frowning.

"Yeah, something like that."

"Listen, Dennis. You've been quite the player. It says here you've been picked up on drug charges before, and carrying a concealed weapon. The last thing you need is another drug bust. You'll do some good time."

Dennis pushed his hands out towards us tied together with the handcuffs.

"Come on man, don't be like that. I ain't mad about the taser."

"The taser and the weed are the least of your problems," said Roberts.

Dennis frowned his eyes at us.

"What's all this about then if it ain't about the weed?"

"It's about Gregg Gelvan," said Roberts.

"Gregg who?"

Dennis leaned back in his chair and pushed his lips out at us.

"I don't know Gregg Melvin," he said.

"Now's not the time to start lying to the police, Dennis," said Roberts. "If you don't start talking some sense to me and real quick, I'm just gonna book you for murder."

Dennis' demeanor changed real quick then. He put his hands up in front of his face as if we'd just thrown him a fastball.

"Hang on now, I didn't kill nobody, and I especially didn't kill Gregg. Man, why didn't you say that?"

"Say what?"

"That Gregg was murdered, that sort of shook my memory awake."

"Right. Start talking, Dennis, real fast."

"Yeah alright, I knew Gregg. We had some business together. You know how it is, two kids from the block."

Roberts closed his folder and stood up.

"I'm done, let's just book him. He's good for it."

"Wait, alright, alright, I'll tell you about Gregg," said Dennis, flapping his hands towards us like he was offering birds of peace. Roberts sat back down.

"I know what your business was, and where you met him. This is your last chance, Dennis, to come clean. He was into you for a ten spot wasn't he?" asked Roberts.

"Nah, he wasn't like that. Gregg was my boy. Yeah, I did some work for him that cost ten Gs. But he'd paid me two already."

"What kind of work did you do?"

"Man, why you gonna be like that. This is off the record right?"

"Nothing's off the record until I say it is. I need to hear your story and I want to hear it now."

"Alright, man. That's harsh. Here's the deal. Gregg wanted to get himself into UCLA so I helped him out with that."

"How?"

"I got him the test results for his grade twelve finals. And then I had a guy take the SATs for him."

"Ten grand seems cheap for all that help," said Roberts.

Dennis nodded and smiled like he was proud to have offered such a deal.

"Gregg was my boy. We went to Locke together. His mother was always good to me, I figured I'd take care of him."

"So you're Mother Teresa," I said.

"Nah man, I ain't saying I didn't make a profit."

"Let's get to the next part where you tell me why you killed him at the pier," said Roberts.

"Man, that's cold. I didn't kill my boy Gregg. I just told you we were friends. But you're right, he was behind with his payments. I was supposed to be paid up by the time UCLA started. So he wanted to meet me at the pier on Tuesday night."

"And did you?"

"Yeah, we met. He told me he was really sorry, he said he was looking for work. He told me he'd get me the money with extra. He said he was gonna give me ten when he only owed me eight. Listen, I was cool with that. I was happy for him. One of us from

Green Meadows was gonna make something of himself. Besides, Gregg had never broken his word. Never. One time we were out joyriding and he took the heat for that one, when it was really me. That's the kind of guy he was."

"What else did you talk about?" I asked.

"He told me he was gonna be a dad. Said he'd met a girl when he'd been shown around the campus in the summer. Said he'd been all confused until he found out she was pregnant. He said it had helped him make sense of everything. He was gonna step up to the plate and do the right thing, and the thing is, he was excited about it. He was looking forward to it."

"I heard he'd promised to get back with Zaira."

"Nah man, he'd told her last weekend that he was moving on. And it was the right thing to do."

"What do you mean?" I asked.

"Man, that Zaira, she's trouble. She didn't want him to head to UCLA. She pretended like she was happy but she wasn't. She's also got a wicked temper. One time they got into this huge fight and she tried to stab him. Hit him in the hand instead. He had to get stitches for it, but told the doctor he'd cut himself on some broken glass. If there's one person who could've killed him it'd be her. And maybe her brothers. They're no good."

"Have you got any evidence to this effect?" asked Roberts.

"I didn't see her kill him if that's what you mean. But get this. I left him around twelve thirty. Like I said, we were good. But when I was leaving I'm pretty sure I saw Zaira hiding behind one of the poles by the roller coaster. It was dark but I'd put money on it being her. I turned around and saw her heading towards Gregg, but I was quite a ways away."

I looked at Roberts and suddenly the coin slipped into the slot and the machine turned its cogs in order. Roberts nodded at me.

"How was Gregg murdered?" asked Dennis.

"He was stabbed."

"Shit, man, didn't I just tell you she tried to stab him one time? I always told him that bitch was crazy, but I guess he was scared of her."

Roberts got up.

"You stay here. Don't go anywhere. An officer will come and get you in a minute."

"But I helped you out right?" asked Dennis.

"Maybe," said Roberts as we opened the door to leave.

"So we're good on the weed, right?"

"What weed?" said Roberts.

Dennis nodded.

"You're alright, man, for a cop."

We left and headed back to Roberts office. He called in Schaal and Campos.

"Cut him loose," he said.

"Just like that?" asked Schaal.

"Just like that, but keep him close. What I want you two to do is get a search warrant for Zaira Estrada's place. Maybe we'll get lucky with the murder weapon still being there."

He said that last part to me. Maybe hell would freeze over. If so, I'd sooner stay in Santa Monica.

"You think she did, boss?" asked Campos.

"Evans said he saw her crouching around the pier when he left Gregg at twelve thirty the night he was murdered. Now she's a small thing, I reckon she would've needed help to move Gregg's body. See if she made any calls to whom and from where. I also want any video or camera footage you can find from the pier that puts her there. I want this buttoned up tomorrow."

"You got it, boss," said Campos, and he and Schaal left.

I looked over at Roberts as he reviewed the file at his desk.

"I suppose we should have seen it coming."

He looked up at me.

"How so?"

"A woman scorned."

"Hell hath no fury like," he smiled. "You quoting Shakespeare again?"

"Actually no, but I see you're misquoting Congreve."

Roberts frowned and shook his head at me.

"Is that right?"

"It sure is. William Congreve wrote 'Heaven has no rage like love to hatred turned, Nor hell a fury like a woman scorned'."

"The point remains."

"It does indeed, seems to me it murdered his remains."

"Sometimes I forget how witty you can be," said Roberts.

"Better a witty fool than a foolish wit," I said, standing up.

"Who's that?"

"That's your boy Shakespeare," I said, turning to leave. "Call me when you haul her in. I want this put to bed nice and tidy like."

"And sung a lullaby?"

"Rather a story of horror, and retribution, and of bodies hanging from gallows."

"I'll see what I can do. Though you know we haven't hanged anyone in over seventy years."

"One can hope," I said, and walked out of the office wondering if capital punishment really was the way to keep us safe from the bogeymen.

Washed Up: Chapter Seven

I didn't think that Roberts would have me called back in to headquarters the rest of the day, and I was right. That meant that Friday morning would be the start of another new day and another paycheck. Two hundred and fifty bucks. I'd get three days pay out of the good citizens of Los Angeles for helping the LAPD solve a case that had really been solved in two days.

My heart was full of gratitude and my head full of cheap beer and even cheaper scotch, when the call came in at nine in the morning.

My tongue felt like it had been replaced with dry coral and my throat felt as if I'd been sucking exhaust from the tailpipe of a Hummer all night. It was John Roberts, and he just wanted to tell me that they were executing the warrant, and he wanted to see if I wanted to attend.

I thanked him most kindly but I asked him to call me when they were bringing her in. Those weren't my exact words but I figured he received the sentiment from the tone.

I got up, showered and shaved and put on some cologne so that I might smell half decent even if I didn't exactly look it. I went to a local diner and had a plate of eggs and bacon with a cup of coffee. I felt shades better. It was a Friday and it started to look like the day might turn out alright after all.

It was noon when Roberts called me up and invited me back to headquarters because they were bringing Zaira in. I wanted a piece of that so I told him I'd meet him there. And I did. I got there before any of the rest of them did. Three interview rooms and three suspects. It seemed like the homicide floor was tailor made for interviewing murder suspects.

Roberts put Zaira in one of the rooms, and Schaal and Campos put Tweedledee and Tweedledum in the other rooms. They came out and we all gathered in the coffee room.

"Carrick and me are gonna take a run at Zaira. You two spar with Pampín and Ezra respectively and see who can get who to break first. The first in a confession will win this day old," said Roberts, pointing to a solitary sugar coated donut in an open, oil stained box.

"Tempting," I said. "Just so we're clear, you want to see who can take the longest time to reach a confession?"

"Smart ass," he said.

Schaal didn't look too impressed and Campos didn't look like he ate many donuts, and me, well I hadn't had lunch and the eggs and bacon had sopped up the last bit of liquor in my belly and I was starting to feel the claws tickle my innards.

"Like old times," I said to him.

Roberts nodded, and we went in to see Zaira and what we could make of this whole debacle. Schaal and Campos sauntered into their interview rooms like men led to the gallows.

Zaira wasn't looking as good as she had the first day I'd met her. She was pretty attractive in a slumming it kind of way, but today her hair was all messed up and she didn't have any makeup on. She did however, look like a killer. How could I tell? Because we practically had her holding the knife on camera. Or as close as you could get to that. I sat down across from her and massaged my temples. I could've used an aspirin, but I what I wanted was a confession. Roberts sat next to me and opened up the ever expanding folder.

"You've been charged with the murder of Gregg Gelvan. All I want to know is why you did it?" asked Roberts.

It was a bold if not steady start. I watched Zaira get her nose all out of joint. She looked at Roberts as if she wanted to burn him with her eyes.

"I told you. I didn't do it. I didn't kill Gregg, okay. He was my boyfriend okay, we were gonna get back together."

"That's what you said the last time we met you," said Roberts.

"'Cause it's true, that's why."

"That's funny because we've heard a different story. Dennis Evans tells us that he thinks you killed Gregg."

"He's a lying no good two bit crook. You gonna believe him over me?"

Zaira tossed her head back in scorn. I wanted to slap some sense and decency into her. What I did was pretend to be the caring uncle.

"Listen," I said, "I know what it's like to be cheated out of something good. To have a chance to make it out of Green Meadows and have a good family in a nice house with a white fence."

"You know nothing."

"I know that I got a chance like Gregg did. I came from West Adams. Only I took my lady with me unlike Gregg."

I looked at her hard trying to seal the deal, see if she'd buy into my lies.

"Lucky for her," she said in a rather condescending tone.

"Lucky for me."

"Zaira, we have you on video at the pier at just before one a.m. arguing with Gregg. We have the knife we found in your bedroom under your bed. And I'll tell you what. Forensics is gonna find Gregg's blood on it. I don't care how careful you think you were in cleaning it, there's always trace. Then, like I said, we have Dennis Evans putting you at the scene of the crime. Lastly, there's the phone call you made to your brothers to help you clean up the mess you made. We found the blood you tried to wash off the pier. The only question is, do you want us to put in a good word. Do you want us to tell the DA that you're remorseful, or do you want to have a chance at the death penalty?"

"Listen," I said, trying again. "I understand what it's like. You've got a chance here to do the right thing and maybe get out of Chowchilla alive. Maybe you can even help out your brothers. Accessory to murder is also a capital offense, especially before the fact like in your case. You want to see them hanged?"

Zaira looked at me, and pouted. Then she put her hands to her mouth and started chewing her nails.

"Ezzy had nothing to do with it. Pampy wouldn't let him go and help me. It was only me and Pampy, okay?"

"All right," I said. "Tell me what happened then."

She looked down and she brushed her hands through her messy hair. When she looked back up, her eyes were swollen with tears.

"I didn't mean it," she said, looking away from me. "I just wanted him for myself. I begged him to come back to me. I told him I loved him, that I was going to support him. He told me it couldn't be. He said that he'd made that bitch pregnant. I couldn't believe it. We'd always talked about starting a family one day, but a couple of months with that bitch and he's gonna have a family with her. No way. We always took precaution, he always wore a rubber, saying it wasn't the time, promising me we'd have a family one day."

Zaira stopped for a moment and squeezed out a couple of her tears. Others took their place in her eyes.

"I took out the knife and I told him he was an asshole. I asked him why he'd played me like that. He said he hadn't meant it, but he'd seen how big the world was now he was going to college, and he told me there was no place there for me. Can you believe it? After all we'd been through, he thought he could just walk away and leave me like garbage on the side of the road. I told him I wasn't going to let that happen. I told him he had to be with me. I told him he'd promised to have a family with me. He said I was overreacting and he told me to put the knife away. When he reached for it I just stabbed him, quickly. Three times. I didn't mean to, it just happened. I tried to help him. I mean it didn't look that bad, he wasn't bleeding lots like you see in the movies. I told him I'd get help so I called Pampy. But by the time he got there, Gregg was dead. What could I do?"

"And what did the two of you do?" asked Roberts.

"Pampy pushed him over the pier and he tried to wipe up the blood. He told me we had to get home, and so he drove me. I didn't want to kill Gregg. But that bitch stole him from me and he couldn't see it. He gets her pregnant and thinks he can just dump me. I'd never been so angry in my life."

I got up and walked out of the interview room. I left Roberts to collect her written statement. She'd write it all down, and maybe that would be cathartic. Maybe that would make it seem all right. But nothing was all right in the world. Gregg's mother had died just this morning. That was the other thing Roberts told me when he called.

God might be watching over the sparrows, but humanity continues to fall off the cliff of life without so much as a murmur. Without even the indifferent sigh of an indifferent God.

About Jason Blacker

Jason Blacker was born in Cape Town but spent most of his first 18 years in Johannesburg. When not grinding his fingers down to stubs at the keyboard he enjoys drinking tea, calisthenics and running. Currently he lives in Canada.

Under his own name he writes hard boiled as well as cozy mysteries, action adventure, thrillers, literary fiction and anything else that tickles his muse. Jason Blacker also writes poetry and daily haikus at his haiku blog.

You can find his haikus and other poetry at his website **www.haiqueue.com**.

To stay up to date and learn about new releases be sure to visit **www.jasonblacker.com** where you can find more information about his writing and upcoming projects.

If you enjoy space opera in the tradition of Star Trek then take a look at Jason Blacker's pen name "Sylynt Storme". It is under the name Sylynt Storme where you can find both sci-fi and vampire fiction written by Jason Blacker.

"Star Sails" is the space opera series and "The Misgivings of the Vampire Lucius Lafayette" is his vampire series.